USA TODAY BESTSELLING AUTHOR

Dale Mayer

HEROES FOR HIRE

ZACK'S ZEST: HEROES FOR HIRE, BOOK 23
Dale Mayer
Valley Publishing Ltd.

ISBN-13: 978-1-773364-08-7
Print Edition

Books in This Series:

About This Book

Zack wasn't someone to focus on his mistakes, but he'd made a big one, and it was hard to move on from it. Still he was determined to work with Levi's team to find new meaning in his life and to get his head on straight. At least that was the plan. When he ends up part of a two-man team to rescue a kidnapped woman, the daughter of a former politician, Zack doesn't know how to react—she's certainly unique. Not the least of which, she didn't appreciate the rescue. … At least not once she learns the details.

Zadie knew her father was guilty of the crimes he'd been accused of. She was more concerned about her mother, who'd always been the downtrodden and obedient wife. But, as more and more evidence shines a light on their lives and her kidnapping, the issue is no longer as clear.

Heartbroken at the losses that keep mounting, Zadie knows she needs a second rescue—hopefully by her same rescuer. Only it's not as simple this time, and it's infinitely more dangerous …

Sign up to be notified of all Dale's releases here!
https://smarturl.it/DaleNews

Prologue

Zack Higgins walked into the coffee shop, took a look around, and realized neither Levi nor Ice were here yet. So he walked to the front counter and ordered himself the largest darkest coffee he could. With that in hand, he turned to look for the most isolated table and found it in the far back right corner of the coffee shop. He headed there and sat down. He tried to get here a few minutes early just because he refused to be late for meetings. He knew the last job had been only okay as far as he was concerned, having dealt with Rebecca. And the case itself had turned out all right, but the end results left him feeling very wounded in many ways.

Even now he still felt stupid, since he hadn't had a sexual relationship with Rebecca in a very long time, and the one that they had been left with for the last many years had been platonic and friendly at best. But because he'd always been hanging on to the wonderment that maybe her daughter was his, his emotional entanglements with Rebecca hadn't been severed. And that was too damned bad because he was sitting here now feeling more than a little sorry for himself, and that was as unacceptable as anything.

"There you are." Ice's warm voice broke through his musings.

He looked up and smiled. "Aren't you a picture," he

1

said, nodding toward her obviously pregnant belly.

"Wow, thanks, I think," she said, sitting down with a hard *thump*. "One day the baby turned, and all of a sudden I look very pregnant. And yet the baby is somehow poking all my organs. So any jokes now are *not* amusing." But her bright laugh that followed belied her words.

He smiled at the two of them, noting that Levi had come up behind him. He stood, shook Levi's hand, and asked, "Are you ready to be a father?"

"Probably not," Levi said amiably. "But, like everything, we learn as we go."

"That's a good way to look at it."

Ice looked to the coffee in front of him and asked, "Did you order anything to eat?"

"No," he said. "The traveling has been pretty rough. I'm here now though."

"Right," Levi said. "What was your analysis of the last job?"

"A shitstorm," he said instantly. "Not the job itself but for the emotional baggage that I had to get rid of."

"And have you now?" Ice asked. "With another month under your belt?"

More than curiosity was in her voice, and he wasn't exactly sure what it was. "I think so," he said with a nod. Then he grimaced and said, "I should have been. Definitely, I know so. But you don't have relationships with people for years like I had with Rebecca and wonder just why you couldn't leave until this stage."

"Good," she said with that compassionate voice he'd heard over the phone many times. "The thing is, none of us heal instantly. None of us get over anything instantly. I'm much encouraged to hear that you are realizing it's a process."

"I wish I could just hit a Delete button on a keyboard," he said. "It would make it a lot easier."

"Maybe," she said. "But the thing is, you need to be free and clear to get your head back into the game."

"As I learned all too recently," he said, staring at the mug of dark brew. "It's a little disturbing to realize just how much I did have to separate from her, when I had already thought those ties were severed." He looked over at Ice and Levi. "What's this meeting all about?"

"Just want to know where you are," Ice said. "Wondering if working for us is still something you're interested in."

"I am," he said, surprised. "I figured after the last job you wouldn't want me."

"Everybody can have a tough job," she said, "and everybody has emotional issues they have to deal with. It's all about how you deal with them that's the problem and/or the solution."

"Are you sure you need more guys?" he asked, studying the two of them, hoping this wasn't some take-pity job. "You've got what? Twenty-four guys working for you?"

"Yes, but we're setting up satellite offices," she said. "One in England, one in Europe."

"Oh." He stopped and stared. "That makes sense. A jump-off point, so to speak, to get your guys' boots on the ground faster around the globe?"

"Plus networking," she said. "And we've been enlisting various companies, like Bullard's, to give us a hand setting those up."

"Well, I'm American," he said, "so I'm not sure just how that'll benefit anybody to have me on board."

"Levi is staying home for the next few months," Ice said,

"and I'm obviously grounded for at least as long."

Zack nodded. "And?" he asked, but there was further silence.

"That means we are also two men short at the compound right now," Levi explained.

"Do you have that much work?"

Ice answered, her tone firm. "Unfortunately, yes."

"Then I'm in," he said. "What can I help you with?"

"When you were in the military, … in the navy," she said, "you worked with Bonaparte and Trent, correct?"

He chuckled. "Absolutely." Then he stopped, looked at them, and asked, "You're not thinking about hiring Bonaparte, are you?"

"Is there any reason not to?" Ice asked.

Zack thought about it, shook his head, and said, "No, I can't say that there is. They are both good men. Bonaparte just came out of a pretty ugly divorce though," he cautioned. "Not sure if he is ready to dive into something like this."

"But he didn't sign up for another tour," Levi said.

"I guess that's something you guys watch for too, isn't it?"

"Let's just say, who is staying in the navy and who's ready to come out are things we are always interested in," Ice said with a smile. "But we also need to vet the men, in particular if we don't know them."

"Got you," Zack said, smiling. "Bonaparte?" he said. "I haven't seen him for a couple years, but he is a really good man, incredibly strong, but I know that the problem with his divorce was that he was *unapproachable*, as he told me."

Levi laughed at that. "I think we've all heard that one time or another."

"Well, I haven't," Zack said. "Apparently, I was wearing

my heart on my sleeve anyway."

"But you're past that now," Ice said. "When you find somebody who would really be a partner in all ways, that relationship will fade into nothing, and you'll wonder what the attraction even was."

"I'm already there," he said. "At least as far as wondering what the original attraction was. I don't have any relationships, so I'm good to go, if you have something of interest."

"I have something of interest," she said, pulling out a thick file from a large bag she had with her and placed it in front of her.

"What's that?"

"Possible recruits," she said. And she opened it.

His picture flashed back at him. "Well, I worked on one job with Galen," he said. "I'd love to try another one."

"Trouble is, we don't do contracts," Levi said. "Either you are in or you are out."

"I think contracts might be the way to go for new recruits, a probationary period of sorts, for both sides," he said slowly, studying the lean-faced man in front of him. Levi had matured a lot over the last couple years. But then he had heavy responsibilities on his shoulders as his company took off into one of the biggest protection agencies around the world. They were known to troubleshoot and to be the guy in a tough corner, when you needed one. "You've built yourself quite a place here," he said to the two of them. They both just nodded. "It must be a little disconcerting to step back for the next few months."

"What else could we do?" she asked. "Out of necessity, we'll be keeping everybody else busy while we reduce our traveling time."

"Understood," he said. He looked as she flipped through

her file. Then he saw Bonaparte's face pop out. "You know he still looks like that too," said. "He's got a real baby face, and so everybody thinks he is this big teddy bear, but, according to his ex-wife, he just was empty emotionally."

"Any reason for that?"

He looked at them in surprise. "His history?"

"I know his sister was murdered a long time ago," Ice said, looking up at him sharply. "Anything else?"

And Zack realized just how important all that history was when it came to hiring those men. He shook his head. "Not that I know of. I was really close to him, back in the day, but haven't seen him but a time or two now over the last couple years."

"We need a four-man team," she said. "Over in Istanbul."

"Turkey?" He stared at her in surprise. "I heard that you guys operated globally. I just hadn't realized how busy you were. As in all over the world."

"I don't know if this will stay in Turkey or not," she said, "but we've certainly covered multitudes of countries by now."

"What's the job?"

She slowly tapped the file, now closed. "The deposed president is under house arrest. As is his vice president," she said. "And the president's daughter has disappeared."

"By choice?"

"It's possible," Levi said, with a nod. "She is thirty-one, and she's a well-known photographer."

"I think I remember something about her," Zack said, staring off into the distance. "Zadie Nather, isn't it?"

"Yes," Levi said. "Zadie Nather. How did you hear about her?"

"She's well-known for publishing very disconcerting photos," he admitted. "Photos about the climate change. Photos about activists. The struggle of the youths to try and regain their position in a world that they consider almost past the turning point. And I think there was something about her father being high up in the government of Turkey *and* very corrupt."

"Exactly," Ice said. "What we don't know is whether her photos are a reason behind her disappearance or whether she disappeared herself because she didn't want to deal with the political climate in Turkey."

"I thought she was operating out of England?" Then he stopped, frowned, looked out the window, and said, "but then I remember something about Australia and the US. She is a Turkish citizen but a vagabond by nature."

"I don't think she has a home base," Levi said. "I think she travels around by boat."

He looked at Levi in surprise. "A houseboat?"

"A small sailing boat," he said. "How do you feel about water?"

He snorted. "I was in the navy. How do you think I feel?"

"You were a Navy SEAL, weren't you?" Ice asked.

He nodded. "I was," a heavy emphasis on the "was."

"Were you caught up in that Commander Dalmatian debacle?"

He nodded. "I was. When bad orders come down, and good guys have to follow them anyway, and the good guys end up in trouble because of following the bad order, well, it got to be a sticky brass political scenario that I didn't like." He said, "I walked. I believe several others walked with me."

Levi nodded. "We try to keep in touch with a lot of

these events," he said, "because that is where a lot of the best men come from."

"Is that how you found out about me?"

"We've had our eye on you for a while," Ice said. Then she winced, and her hand immediately went to her belly. She started to deep breathe. Levi looked over at her, an eyebrow raised. She slowly shook her head. "No, he's just arguing for lack of space."

"He?" Zack asked.

She looked at him, smiled, and said, "That's my guess."

He grinned. "I can't imagine that it would make a difference to either of you," he said warmly.

"Hell no," Levi said. "Better she has twins, and we are done with it right away."

"I'll suck at that," she said.

"Be pretty rough for the first few years though," Zack warned. "A friend of mine had twins, and all she did was diapers for a while."

"Well, we do have friends at home just dying to get their hands on the baby," Levi said. "So Ice will have to fight to get her own diaper-changing time."

Zack grinned at that. He'd heard so much about the compound and its family environment that he couldn't imagine any child growing up there would be anything but well loved by many aunts and uncles. It was sheer magic that they managed to make it work at all. "So either I'm in or out?" he asked abruptly.

"You're in," Levi said. He stood. "At the bare minimum, get some zest back into your life."

"Well, put that way, how can I refuse?"

Chapter 1

ZACK WALKED THROUGH the airport and out into the city. He stopped and inhaled the air, taking in the scent that was uniquely Istanbul. He had visited here in the past, yet the city's color scheme still enthralled Zack with its rich and vibrant hues. This lifestyle he hadn't explored during his last visit, and he doubted he would have time to now.

Behind him, a man called out, "Stop your daydreaming."

Zack smiled, knowing before he even saw him, it was his friend Bonaparte. His French accent gave him away. Zack turned, smiled to see his old friend again, and walked into his hug. That was the thing about Bonaparte; he was another hugger, like so many of his countrymen.

Bonaparte motioned toward a car parked off to the side of the road. "Come on. I'm double-parked. You know how that will go down here." They raced to the vehicle and hopped in, taking off before authorities came over to pound on the hood of the car.

Zack laughed. "Still breaking the rules, I see? You haven't changed one bit."

"No," Bonaparte said, humor clear in his voice. "I only break the rules when they don't work for me."

At that, Zack's laugh became uncontrollable. Damn! He hadn't laughed like this in a long time. "I don't know how that'll work out for us here," he said, finally catching his breath. "But damn, it's good to see you."

"It's always good to see you," Bonaparte said with a rolling laugh.

"Any further intel on this case?"

"Levi texted me a few minutes ago, telling me that he'd uploaded the updated case file for us."

Immediately Zack pulled out his phone and brought up the email and downloaded the file. "I still don't understand why he thinks this is the point of origin from where she'd gone missing."

"Her passport cleared customs ten days ago, entering Turkey. They think she came back to see her folks."

"Aren't they both in exile under guard?"

"Yes."

"So she made it to their side and then what?"

"According to what the parents told Levi, Zadie went out for a walk in the garden. She was talking on her phone, last they saw her, only she didn't return."

"And they, of course, called out a warning and asked for help?"

"No, not initially," Bonaparte continued. "They thought she'd found a way to sneak out."

"Why would she have to sneak?"

"Because it was made clear that, once she arrived, she was under house arrest as well."

Zack stopped, froze, looked at him, and said, "Seriously?"

Bonaparte nodded grimly. "According to the parents— and this is just the little bit of information that they've managed to get out—Zadie had no intention of staying as a prisoner with them. So, when she disappeared, they initially congratulated themselves, thinking that she had found a way to get out from under house arrest. But, when they hadn't heard from her in the last four days, they got worried."

"How did Levi get involved?"

"I believe it came through Bullard," Bonaparte said. He twisted to look at Zack. "I know the name, but I've never met the man."

"I see."

"But I know that Bullard and Levi work together a lot," Bonaparte added grimly. "Is it just the two of us?"

"Yes," Zack said.

"I thought this was supposed to be a four-man team?"

Zack shook his head. "Not unless two more guys shake free from their ops and can help us out here. Plus there is the travel delay to consider. So consider us on our own for this one."

The vehicle jerked to the side quickly, sending Zack lurching against him. "I see your driving hasn't improved," he said with a laugh. Bonaparte's driving was akin to a race car let loose on the autobahn. And that included zigzagging through the traffic to get where he was going, completely ignoring any road signs, of which there were very few anyway.

"If people would just get out of my way," Bonaparte said, unfazed, "life would be a lot easier."

"I don't think that's how the traffic works," Zack retorted.

"Well, it should," he said. "It would all work much easier that way."

Zack chuckled. "Says you. The rest of the people probably think you are a crazy idiot they should shoot."

Bonaparte shrugged and moved between two other vehicles across two lanes, simultaneously hitting an exit at top speed. The thing was, he was such a skilled driver that at no time did Zack feel like his life was in danger. But he could imagine how everybody else on the road felt.

Zack pulled up the file on Zadie, but it had just a few more details, not a whole lot. "She's never been married and has no children," he commented.

"No, her political activist aspirations kept her single apparently."

"Or she just didn't like the political aspirations of the men around her."

"Same thing." Bonaparte looked at him. "What about you? You never married?"

"Nope," Zack said with delight. "Still single."

"What about kids?"

His heart twitched at that; then he shook his head. "No, no children either."

"I've got the two, as you know," Bonaparte said, "but the wife has them, and she already remarried."

"What about you?" Zack asked, looking at the big man in surprise. "Visiting rights?"

"I get them on holidays," he said, giving his partner a fat grin, "and, boy, do we like to holiday."

"I can imagine. So something like Levi's place might be good for you now."

"Yes, and I'll take off all my holidays so I can be with the kids."

"That sounds pretty cool," he said. "How old are they now?"

"Eight and six," Bonaparte said with a nod of satisfaction. "The perfect age to start doing things together. They want to learn how to surf next summer."

"It's a good age for them to learn too." Zack felt momentary twinges, as he realized that he had nobody to teach or to spend holidays with doing things like that. Nobody to even share the world. He shook his head. "You are very lucky."

"In many ways, yes," Bonaparte said. "The wife and I are at least amicable."

"Yet you don't call her your ex?"

"Mostly for the kids' sake," he said. "We tried the first-name thing. The kids didn't like that either."

"Dictated by the children, huh?"

Bonaparte gave a big shrug and said, "You do what you got to do to keep the peace." He took another hard right and sent the car careening in the opposite direction.

"We are not being followed or anything, are we?"

"Nope," Bonaparte said. "But I had enough time to beat that light, so I took it."

"Right," Zack said, settling back into his seat. "I see little new in this updated file. Basically nobody knows anything."

"Well, there is an interesting part to that though. Her passport wasn't cleared leaving through any customs checkpoint. So she didn't leave the country by air or train or bus."

"Doesn't mean she didn't drive or walk across the border," he said. "She could have taken a boat, and wasn't she used to traveling that way anyway?"

"The boat is in England," he said.

"Right, but we have to figure this out. Was she kidnapped, and, if so, by whom and why?"

"The biggest one being the why," he said. "We are almost there."

Zack peered into the night, the darkness slowly taking over. "The perfect time for an ambush."

"Or a perfect time for surveillance," Bonaparte said in his suspicious tone of voice. "And that's exactly what we are up to," he said.

ZADIE ROLLED OVER once again and huddled tighter. Her arms, her knees, her hands curled up in the tightest ball as possible. Zadie stared at the tiny room she was in and wondered how the hell her life had come to this. But then, every person who found themselves in prison unexpectedly must feel the same way.

Day four of captivity and still on the property where her parents were being held—or at least she assumed she was, but she didn't know for sure—blew her away. She'd been out for a walk, trying to set up her plans to escape the sudden house arrest she found herself under. Only to be grabbed when she hit the trees. She'd deliberately gone along that route, checking the guards' timing. Just when she had seen a chance to escape the guards, someone else had nabbed her.

So it wasn't the house arrest guards who had taken her. It wasn't the same people who were holding her parents that had grabbed her. And wasn't that just something? Of course Turkey was in a political turmoil, what with all the factions fighting one another to take over as the ruling body. Even without all that going on, her father had made a lot of enemies. She was barely on talking terms with her father at all, but, for her mother, Zadie would do a lot.

And her mother's health seemed to be failing, from little slips her mother had said about doctors and such. Sounded as if her mother needed medical attention, and she was unlikely to get the necessary care while she was under guard herself. If her parents had been left in exile, that's one thing, but for the new government regime to keep them prisoner was something else entirely.

The new leader was also likely to prosecute her dad for crimes committed while he'd been in office. She didn't know if he was innocent; she doubted it. Still, it was the perfect action of the new government to ensure that the old one couldn't come back into power.

She shivered some more, knowing that her body was burning through every meager calorie her captors supplied, just to stay warm. She had already been lean, having practiced martial arts for a long time. Too bad she hadn't kept it up.

She thought about her kidnapping, wondering if she could have done anything to prevent it. But they had used the element of surprise to drug her and to take her down.

An odd smell still remained on her skin and her breath, which her stomach hadn't liked either. She had upchucked as soon as she'd initially woken up in her cell. Thankfully she made it to a bucket close by, but days later she still wasn't doing well. And, while she slept that first night, her captors had removed the bucket. Which just meant that more drugs were in her system than she was aware of because she hadn't woken up much since being jailed. Maybe the drugs themselves were part of the reason why she was so cold too.

Outside her cell she heard voices. She noted one window high up, with bars on the inside. Her door was solid with no windows or slits at all. She already knew that it would be useless to cry out, and the voices were from those who had no care for her. She didn't even know why she was being held.

When a key clinked in the lock to the door, she forced herself to sit up, hugging her knees against her chest. She saw the tray come in first, and she hated the fact that she was so eager to get the food that she could forget everything else. But when two people came in, one in a white overcoat, she frowned. "Are you here to give me more drugs or something to stop me from freezing?" she said thickly, her tongue swollen and hard to operate.

The doctor immediately walked over and checked her vitals. "She is really sick," he said to his companion. "She must have reacted to the drugs you gave her."

The other man shrugged. "So what? It doesn't matter."

"It matters," the doctor said. "If she dies on us, you will not get what you want either."

"I'm not sure we should have taken her anyway," her guard said. "Would have been better if we'd taken her parents."

"Nobody cares about the parents either," the doctor said. "This is another foolish venture of your brother's." At that, the guard glared at him. But the doctor shrugged and added, "You know I'm right."

"He wants to get our father out of jail," the guard said. "You can't fault us for that."

"By imprisoning another woman?" The doctor shook his head. "Especially this one. She is nothing but trouble. All you have to do is a Google search to see that!"

The analysis of her life up 'til now came down to those few short words. *Nothing but trouble.* "Is that all you think of me?" she asked. "I spent my life fighting injustice. And now I'm in the heart of it all."

"And yet your father is the most corrupt," her guard snapped.

She stared up at him. "I haven't had anything to do with my father in many, many years. He was only president of the country for four years and leader of his party for two before that," she said. "I haven't lived at home for twelve, if not fourteen years by now," she snapped back. "Are all children to blame for the sins of the father?"

"That's what it says in the Bible," the doctor said smoothly. He finished his tests and turned to the guard. "She needs something to warm her up. The drugs are having a terrible effect on her. She needs blankets, and she needs more clothing. Put that food down and go get her something," he ordered.

The guard glared at him.

"She is too sick to even fight me off. Go."

At that, the guard reluctantly lowered the tray to the floor and turned, but he locked them in as he left.

She stared at the doctor. "Thanks for that much, at least," she said, her teeth chattering.

He looked at her, frowning. "I meant what I said. You are no good to us dead."

"Apparently I'm no good to you alive either," she said, shaking her head. "I don't understand why they would even kidnap me."

"Prisoner exchange," he said. "But I don't think they chose their prisoner very well."

She stared at that. "Who is running the show?" she asked. "And how long before I find out if it's a deal or not?"

"I can't tell you," he said. "You might as well settle in for the ride. It will be a long one."

He straightened when the door opened, and the guard walked back in, carrying a stack of blankets. He threw them at her. A large oversize hoodie was on top of it all. She immediately snatched that and pulled it over her head, tucking her knees up underneath. "I don't suppose you brought any socks, did you?" And she pointed to her feet, turning blue.

He grumbled and disappeared but came back a little later with what appeared to be men's socks. They had holes in them, but she took them. "Thank you," she said gratefully, as she put them on. They came almost up to her knees. But it covered her feet, and that was what was important.

With the hoodie on, the socks, and the blanket wrapped around her, she just might survive. The doctor and the guard left. She leaned over to look at the tray they brought in. It appeared to be soup, a sandwich, and a cup of something. And now she didn't have to worry about the food being drugged, what with her negative reaction to them. She was damn grateful to have the food. All she had to do was figure out how to get the hell out of here. She pulled out her phone and checked it, but she still had no bars to send a message. Probably why they let her keep her phone. They knew she could never use it.

Making as little movement as possible so she'd keep the blankets in place and the heat wrapped around her as much as she could, she pulled the tray onto her knees and settled back to enjoy her first meal in a long time.

Chapter 2

A FTER ZADIE FINISHED eating, she put the tray on the floor and crawled up on the bed, pulling as many blankets as she could over the top of her head. She laid here, waiting. Afterward she pulled out her phone and started to write. She wrote down her experience since the beginning of her kidnapping. She took several photos to describe anything and everything that she could. She really wanted photos of her guard and the doctor. Somehow she had to take those when they weren't looking.

Just then the windowless door opened again, and the guard came back. She had her phone off to the side, hidden under the folds of the blanket, so he couldn't see it. Angling it as well as she could, she continued to snap photos, hoping that he didn't notice as he bent down, picked up the tray, and walked out without saying a word. Quickly she pulled the phone back up and studied the pics that she took. A couple good ones were here but only one shot of his profile, and one showed his face slightly in shadows. But then she clicked on the last one and smiled.

"There you are," she whispered. Knowing that she still had no way to get the messages out to anyone, she opened up emails and quickly prepared as many of the emails as she could with the photos attached, explaining her circumstances.

Regardless, she knew that, if she escaped, or if her phone ever connected with cell service, someone would get her messages. Stuck as she was down in this dark basement, chances were it wouldn't happen until they moved her, which meant she also had to keep her phone hidden. She sure didn't want to remind them that she had her cell.

She thought about that for a long moment and then tucked the phone inside her sock, under her pants leg. With her socks pulled up over the bottom of that leg, she hoped her phone would remain with her.

Not ideal but it was something. She lay quiet, grateful to be warm, when she heard the voices again. Frowning, she slipped out of bed and made her way to the door, wishing she knew exactly what her captors were up to. She strained at the words. A bit of English and a bit of Ukrainian she thought, or a Turkish dialect she didn't know. However, most she could understand.

"How long are we keeping her?"

"I don't know what the plan is," her guardsman said, recognizing his voice.

"I think it's foolish," said someone else, a woman.

"That's enough out of you," her guard snapped.

They spoke in hushed tones after that, but the argument raged on. Zadie wondered if she could use that to her advantage. Maybe find an opportunity to cause further disharmony between her captors.

She needed a chance to get a message to someone. A window in the wall revealed some light outside, but the window was superhigh up, and her bed was chained against the wall. So she couldn't twist the bed frame, lift it, or turn it in any way to give her a boost up there. And, as long as people were outside her door, if she could move the bed, they would definitely hear her.

Sighing, she looked at the bars on the window and the glass behind it. She had to try. Would she have another chance to escape? She made a running leap to jump up the wall and to grab at the bars with her hands. Surprisingly she caught them. As her body slammed into the cement, she shuddered at the pain.

She managed to pull herself up. As such, she rested ever-so-slightly on the wide windowsill. The wall was made out of thick concrete, enough so that she could rest her body weight upon the ledge. She studied outside, noting the windows were at ground level. So she was in a basement. Although a window was here, the glass itself she could get through but not with these bars on the inside, which was why they had locked her in here, she assumed.

She studied the grounds outside, wondering if she truly was in the same place as her parents. It looked similar, but that wasn't any guarantee. She could be at any one of the neighboring estates as well. Hell, she could be in a neighboring country.

Finally unable to hang on any longer, she awkwardly dropped to the floor.

With her knee scraped and her body more bruised than she expected, she slowly limped her way back to the bed, where she pulled up the blankets around her. She curled up on the tin cot as the door opened suddenly. She startled in surprise and stared up to see a woman glaring at her. "Who are you?" Zadie asked quietly.

The woman motioned with her hand to be quiet. "I don't want you here," she snapped. "I don't think you should be here."

"Then let me go," Zadie said.

DALE MAYER

The woman shook her head. "I can't do that."

"Then I can't help you," Zadie said, the cold and fatigue hitting her again. Just that effort of looking out the window had exhausted her. "I'm hurt. I'm sick, and I'll die on you in here."

"And that might be the best." The woman nodded.

Zadie stared at her. "Are you so heartless?"

"No," she said, "but I'm a survivor. This is a foolish venture."

"Do you love him?" Zadie asked with insight.

The woman just glared at her.

Zadie nodded. "Yes, you do. Otherwise you wouldn't do this."

"Not this one," she said. "His brother is my husband."

"And I'm sorry then. That means your father-in-law is the one in jail. Is he Turkish too?"

Surprise lit the dark depths of the other woman's gaze. "Yes. You know about that?"

"I understand that's why your brother-in-law is doing this," she said, "but I don't know why holding me makes any difference."

"Not only won't it make a difference," she said, "it shouldn't make a difference. His father is bad news."

"So why does he want him free?"

"He doesn't believe that he is bad news," she replied sadly.

"Then help me get loose," Zadie retorted. "Let me go. Otherwise that monster will be free too."

"I can't let you go," the woman responded. "He would know who helped you."

"So we make it look as if the doctor did it."

The woman stared at her in surprise.

22

Zadie shrugged. "Surely that would be easier to do than have you be responsible."

The woman stared out across the window and shook her head. "No," she said, "there is no place for you to go."

"You let me worry about that," Zadie said slowly, leaning up so that she sat against the back wall, and she studied the woman's face. "I promise I won't come back here."

"No," the woman said, "you won't, but you'd send somebody."

"But I don't have anybody," Zadie said. "You know that."

"Your parents."

"They are prisoners in their own right," Zadie said harshly. "I made the mistake of coming to see my mother, who may be very ill."

The woman stared at her in surprise. "We heard nothing about this. Why didn't we?"

"It won't make the news," Zadie said with a wave of her hand. "You know what that's like. They don't want anybody to play on their sympathies."

"This is true." She turned abruptly, headed out the door, and called back quietly, "I will think on it," slamming the door hard behind her.

Zadie sank back on the bed. She'd done what she could; she didn't think it would be enough, but it was a start. It was actually a chink in their armor. Maybe, just maybe, Zadie could make that work.

"DO WE HAVE any idea if they snatched her from the property?" Zack asked.

"The satellite only gave us vague details of vehicles coming and going, nothing showing where they snatched her."

"No tracker anywhere to identify her on the move?"

"She has her phone supposedly, but we are not getting a trace on it."

"Is that because it's not turned on or because it's not traceable?"

"Let's just say it's not coming up anywhere."

"But the tracing is still ongoing, correct?"

Bonaparte nodded. "Correct. It's possible her phone is dead, or she is someplace where there is no reception. No way to track her."

"Makes sense if she was a prisoner."

"Any chance she is still in the same place?"

"Of course there is a chance," Zack said, "but she could just as easily have been moved."

"So we need a better way to track her then."

"Yes, we do."

"Door to door?"

"That will take too long," Zack said with a shake of his head.

"Deliveries? Too many vehicles at one spot, something to track activities at any particular house?" Bonaparte asked.

"We are working on that," he said. "What we do have is the estimated time of her kidnapping. We have two delivery trucks and a landscape company coming and going from their property where the parents are under house arrest."

"So we start there," Bonaparte said.

"Already started," Zack said.

"We'll be boots on the ground, set up a moving perimeter, a continuous watch at the property for the first few hours," Bonaparte stated, "to make sure nothing is going on there that we don't know about. Meanwhile Levi can get the rest of his crew to do the background checks and figure out what's going on by tracking and cross-referencing the employees at the estate."

"I think Zadie's disappearance is related to that place."

"Fine," Bonaparte said. "We'll stash the car a mile away and get us both fitted."

"Good enough." Zack checked his phone for satellite imagery and brought up the layout of the property. "The residence has a fair number of trees, lots of coverage."

"Yes, but we need to be in a position where we can actually do something, in case we see something important," Bonaparte reminded him.

He nodded, zoomed in on the image, and added, "Even along this back entrance, there are quite a few trees. It's a huge property."

"Close to twelve acres," Bonaparte said. "And that will be the problem. Because we could block ourselves into a corner and may miss whatever is happening on the other side."

"A four-man team would have been good about now, but it's just the two of us, so we'll keep our comms open, and our surveillance moving." Zack frowned. "You are hardly a size to hide."

"In the dark," he replied humorously, "I'm just a bigger shadow." And he gave Zack a big fat grin. "Besides, they won't really see my size until they are too close."

"If you say so," he said. "More satellite will be good, along with getting suited up." And by that he meant armed. And, with darkness having settled in, Zack headed to the back corner of the property, while Bonaparte took the front corner.

They would head in opposite directions on a slow patrol

that should last one hour around all twelve acres. That wasn't exactly a slow patrol. But, considering that they had to cut through some of that acreage to go behind the house and then check out the front yard, that process meant for a shorter overall distance.

As soon as Zack got into position, he set himself up some pointers to sort out his location. Being in the middle of darkness made it easy to lose track. He checked on the stars, oriented himself securely, checked on the horizon to make sure he knew what it would look like from this spot, all the way around, then headed along the back of the property.

A fence surrounded the house, and this surprised him greatly. But then maybe that was just a standard around there. If they had domesticated animals, that made sense, but he highly doubted that here. Maybe this property was picked as a good place for house arrest because of that fence.

Zack headed slowly toward Bonaparte's position. He heard various birds moving in the night. He thought a bat flew close to his ear. Wasn't too much of a surprise, particularly now, as they would swoop down in the night, looking for bugs. As Zack made his way from tree to tree, outside of Mother Nature, there wasn't a sound.

He really wanted to get up to the house. After he'd done three revolutions of the property, he sent a message to Bonaparte, saying that, on the next round, he would check out the base of the house.

Bonaparte sent back a question mark.

Zack just sent him a thumbs-up. By the time Zack reached the point where he would break their patrol, he slipped into the yard, using as much of the tress and the landscape as he could to cover his tracks, and made it up against the house.

He knew from their intel that the parents were being held upstairs, and he knew that there were guards. He had seen several of them out in the front, but nobody was patrolling the property. A large veranda entrance was at the rear of the house, and he'd seen several people come out to have a smoke, tossing the butts onto the brick walkway and going back inside.

He skipped along the edge so he completely merged into the brick base of the house. The first twelve feet were all brick; after that, it appeared to be a combination of brick and maybe stucco or adobe. He wasn't exactly sure what the differences were in this part of the world.

There were windows at ground level but not too many. He crept all the way around and saw four different windows he could easily access, one on each side of the house. But someone had boarded up three of them. The fourth one appeared to be glass, but he couldn't see inside. It was too dark. Even giving his pupils time to adjust, Zack still could see nothing. He made his way back to the boarded-up windows and pulled off one piece of rotten wood to check behind it. And again found nothing to see. Except that the glass was broken. With the boards completely removed, and, using his sleeve to cover his hand, he removed some broken glass so he could look inside. If nothing else, it was a way to get the daughter out of here.

He quickly sent several photos back to Bonaparte. He sent a message back, asking if Zack was going in. With an affirmative answer, he cleared enough of a space through the broken glass window that he could creep inside and pulled the wood back across the hole. Then he jumped to the floor. He could hear rustling in the basement, probably rats and mice living down here. He quickly did a walk around, holding out his arms to check the size of the room. It was small, maybe ten by twelve, and then he found the door.

With the door opened, he slipped out into a hallway. He stopped to give his eyes a moment to adjust, but it was sheer darkness down here. He could see shadows in the walls, recessed to show other rooms, but nobody appeared to be here. No lights were on.

He heard music drifting down from upstairs, but no further sounds were down here. Just to be sure, he did a quick search and got to the next room—empty—where a second boarded window was, and the glass was broken too. The third boarded window was to yet another empty room. Two of the windows had bars on the inside of the windows.

As he rounded the fourth side of the house, he came up against a locked door. He turned the handle, but it wouldn't budge. He heard a noise on the other side. But no window was in the door. He waited a few minutes and then whispered, "Hello?"

To his shock and amazement, a woman whispered back, "Hello?"

Chapter 3

ZADIE HAD NO clue who was there. But if it was anybody other than her guard, she'd take it. "Who's there?" she asked in her native tongue then repeated it in English, her tone low and short.

"Are you Zadie?"

"Yes," she cried out in surprise.

"I'm here to rescue you," he said.

She shook her head in surprise. "How did you even know I was missing? I haven't reached anyone."

"Your parents."

She leaned against the door in relief. "There's a guard, his brother-in-law, and a sister-in-law involved," she said. "I don't know who they are but saw her in the kitchens where my parents are being held. They kidnapped me from the grounds of the estate. I don't have any cell service down here."

"That's fine," he said. "I'm trying to open your door."

"It's locked," she warned. She stepped back as she heard something at the door. There was a sudden *click*, and then the door opened. She turned her phone on and held the faint light up to see her rescuer, a stranger. "Thank you," she whispered.

He stared at her, letting her shine the light on his face. Then he said, "We don't have time for this." Up above they heard footsteps and people coming down the stairs. He swore and said, "I've got to go."

"I'll stay here," she said. "Just don't forget me."

He stepped out of the way into the closest room where she watched him leave, knowing she'd never get the door locked again. She quickly closed it, knowing he needed time to get away immediately. With the door closed, she sat back down again, wondering if they would notice that the door wasn't locked.

She curled up in bed, wondering what else might have caused them to come check on her. When the door burst open, she acted as if she'd just woken up in surprise. Lights flashed on her and then around the room. "What's the matter?" she asked, struggling to sit up, rubbing her eyes.

"Nothing," her guard said, and he stepped outside, slamming and locking the door again behind him.

She heard him downstairs doing a sweep, and she had no idea if her rescuer had found a good hiding place or not. The fact he had found her said he had some skills. But were they enough?

Anxious, she waited for someone to return. Outside she heard the guards yelling back and forth. "Nobody is here. False alarm." She had no clue what noise could possibly have alerted anybody. Then she heard someone speaking about somebody walking outside. She wondered about that too.

She listened intently as the footsteps all went back upstairs. And it seemed an interminably long time before a scratching noise came on her door again. She crept over and whispered, "Hello?"

"It's me. Stand back." He unlocked the door again, standing there like a badass.

She stared at him in shock. "How did they miss you on

the search?"

He smiled and said, "Come on. Let's go."

"I have no shoes or coat."

"Grab one blanket," he said.

She quickly snatched up a blanket, wrapped it around her, and, leaving the door closed, as if locked, followed him silently through the basement, only able to see him in front of her. The rest of the floor was so dark; it was void of light. When they got to another room, he spoke again. "This window is broken and doesn't have bars. I will lift you up, and you go through the window and wait for me on the other side."

Before Zadie had a chance to make a sound, he boosted her up and popped her through. She fell out of the small window ledge onto the grass below. Immediately she untangled herself from the blanket. The blanket had stopped her from getting cut; by the time she had the blanket off and on her feet, he stood beside her.

He quickly tossed the blanket back inside and replaced the wood that covered the broken window. "Now," he said, "we have to be beyond careful."

She looked at him in surprise.

"We have absolutely no cover from here to the tree line," he replied to her look. "This is where it gets dicey."

She whispered in a low voice, "They saw someone outside. That's how they knew that somebody was probably inside."

"No," he corrected. "That's how they *worried* somebody might have been inside. Now we have to make sure we get you away from here before they can confirm it."

She looked back. "I should have brought the blanket with me."

"No, don't worry about it. They'll know soon enough how we got you out."

She winced at that. "Do we just run as fast as we can?"

"How tired are you?"

"I'm exhausted and terrified," she said. "However, believe me. When it comes time, I'll be able to run, just not too far."

He pointed to a series of trees, about one hundred yards away. "Can you make it there?"

She looked up to see a flashlight shining above. He immediately pulled her flat against the house and held a finger against her lips. He pointed to a cloud moving across the sky. "When the moon goes dark, we will go like bats out of hell," he murmured.

She nodded, her breath caught at the back of her throat as she watched the clouds drift across the moon. She could hear him counting down beside her.

"Four, three, two, one, go." And they raced into the night.

Zadie ran as hard and as fast as she could. The cold basement room she had endured over the last few days—plus her lack of food—had already taken a lot of her energy, but the panic she felt at being recaptured lit a fire to her heels. She stumbled several times, but her savior always pulled her forward again until she regained her feet. By the time they reached the trees, her head pounded, and pain seized her chest as it tried to rise and fall. She struggled to catch her breath. Collapsing to the ground, Zadie rolled to her side, pulled her knees against her chest, and gasped for air. "Did we make it?"

"I'm checking," he said.

She watched as he peered through the trees back at the

house. The same house her parents were in. She couldn't believe she was still here, still in the same damn place. Were they okay? Was her mother okay? From where she lay, it seemed the same. She needed to get out of here, make a new plan, and see how to get her mother out of her prison, possibly with the help of this new guy. Her previous plan would no longer work, what with the house-arrest guards and now this inner element of kidnappers involved, all at the same house.

She understood the two brothers wanted to get their father out of jail, but, according to the one woman, the father was somebody who shouldn't come out of jail. It made little sense why they kidnapped Zadie when she was already a captive. But, as usual, more than one game plan was happening here, involving different political ideologies, she presumed. She lay on the ground, wondering if her body would ever feel normal again. For all the debilitating cold she experienced inside, a weird numbness now spread up her legs.

Finally her rescuer dropped beside her and asked, "Are you okay? We have to get out of here."

"I'm okay," she lied. "Help me to my feet."

He reached down, she clasped his forearms, and he helped her up. "We will go around the back," he said. "We can't risk staying here any longer."

"I know," she said. "They have some sentries around, and another two guards were looking after me, but also a woman is with the two jailers. I don't think she would come outside."

"They will have more men around. Let's go."

She did her best, really she did. She thought she was in great shape physically, but he was moving too fast, too steadily ahead of her. Even with her best efforts, she fell behind.

Immediately he corrected his pace, and he whispered, "Come on. You can do this." He reached out a hand, and she grabbed on, as if it were a lifeline.

"Says you," she said. "Where the hell are we going anyway?"

"Off this property into a couple estates on the other side. I'm not out here alone. I do have a partner. We have a vehicle not too far away."

At the sound of a getaway car, she almost cried with relief. Every step was bone jarring. "I'm not feeling too well," she gasped. The stitch in her side made it difficult to breathe.

He slowed his pace to a walk, and she bent over double, gasping for breath. "It's hard when you go past the normal pace," he said. "We have to get your breathing back down, before we can speed up again."

She just nodded.

He kept walking, nudging her forward, not allowing her to stop longer than a few seconds. She really needed a ten- or a fifteen-minute break, but she understood why she couldn't have it. She said, "Are we going straight to the vehicle?"

"In a roundabout fashion," he responded. He pulled out his phone and quickly sent several messages as he kept walking. "Damn it."

He seemed to be one of those incredibly solid people who could continuously multitask. She knew she texted better when she was stationary or sitting down. She marveled at all those people who could do it while walking or even running. For her, doing such would have caused her to fall.

When his phone vibrated, he nodded with satisfaction. "We are confirmed to meet a couple estates over," he said.

"It's not far, about two miles."

"Why can't they pick us up here?"

"Because the two of us are here on the property," he said. "We parked the vehicle so it was hidden from view near the house."

"Two miles is a long way," she said.

He looked at her, concerned. "Did they beat you?"

"No. Starved, yes. And drugged. I'm still dealing with those aftereffects."

Understanding whispered across his face. "I'll see if he can find a closer rendezvous point." Even as they talked, he quickly sent off a text.

She was grateful and said, "We need probably what? A half hour to go two miles?"

"At least," he said. "If we were running, we could do it in fifteen minutes, but, if you can't run, then we'd be hard-pressed to walk it in that time."

"So let's go," she said bravely.

He picked up the pace slightly, and she caught him glancing at her several times in concern. She thought she'd been doing better, keeping up fine.

Then he said, "This isn't working." He bent down and picked her up.

She gave out a small shriek as she was suddenly airborne. He was carrying her at a run, and she was no lightweight. She was 130 at least.

He started to jog now.

"Good Lord," she said. Her arms went around his neck, as she hung on tightly, trying to stop the jostling. For whatever reason, it was killing her. Racking pain ran up and down her body. But she pursed her lips and hung on.

"It's the only way to get there in time," he said.

"Nothing closer?"

"Nothing doable," he murmured. "Just hang on, and this will be over soon."

"If you say so. How is it you can even do this?" she whispered. She could sense the effort he was putting in, and his body was already streaked with sweat as he carried her. "I'm so sorry," she said. "I wish I could do more."

That startled a laugh out of him. "Don't be," he said. "If you were on my back, it'd be a different story. Carrying you like this is a little harder."

"I can go on your back, if that's easier?"

"Maybe," he said. "I'll let you know. In the meantime, I'll keep going this way."

"But you can hardly see," she said. "I can barely see anything." Indeed, her vision had closed down to a light gray everywhere. She closed her eyes and clenched them tight as she tried to catch her breath. If she could at least do that much, she could regain her feet and run beside him. "I used to run," she said, "but I haven't in the last few years."

"Not an issue," he said. "Let's just keep moving."

And though the pain still racked her, she buried her face against his neck and hung on. He had that raw male smell to him, mingled with sweat, some kind of aftershave she thought, topped off with a bit of beard bristle. She wanted to nuzzle in closer, but, when she moved in closer, she would then bounce back again.

"I'm sorry if this is hurting you," he said. "You never did say if you were hurt in any way."

"I don't think so," she said, "but the cold is just killing me. They said it was a reaction to the drugs, and maybe it was. I don't know, but it was also a reaction to a lack of food and to the housing that they put me into."

"That bare room?"

"Yes. And, yes, I had blankets," she said, "but they only just gave those to me. Before that, I was alone on that cot with nothing to cover up with."

"And that's a good way to get sick," he said. His breathing hardly appeared affected, even though he was jogging as he carried her.

"I know," she said. "I didn't think I'd ever get warm again. And honestly, I wasn't really. I asked them for socks, and they gave me some. They were a help, but I caught a chill, and I couldn't shake it."

He nodded. "We should have brought the blanket with us."

"No," she said, "it's all good." At least she hoped it was because this was even more painful as time went on.

A few minutes later, he whispered, "We are almost there. Hold tight."

She let out a gasp of relief.

He glanced at her sharply. "Are you sure you are not hurt?"

She shook her head. "I'm sure." But, after this bumpy ride, something was jarring loose, she was sure of it. It seemed as if every part of her body had taken a beating. She didn't understand it, but then she'd never experienced being carried like this before either. Hell, she didn't remember ever being carried.

Even as a child, it wasn't as if she had a father figure who took time to play with her in any way. Her father had always been a political demon, heading upward at all costs. It was good for his image to have children, so he had one. But he didn't waste his time on her. Zadie's relationship had been entirely with her mother, and, even if her father was shot and hung, Zadie would do what she could to save her mother because her mother was innocent in all this.

Wasn't she?

Zadie had to believe that. When she got her mother safely away, they would have an honest heart-to-heart, and Zadie could figure out how involved her mother had been in her father's illegal political activities. Despite the slip-ups her mother let by, Zadie was happy that at least her mother appeared to be fine and healthy when she'd seen her. The kidnappers hadn't shown any interest in her parents at all—as if realizing trying to kidnap the pair of them while under guard was more than the kidnappers could do. Plus they were aging and not in the best physical shape. *Go for the daughter* appeared to be their motto.

Her mother's mistake had been marrying a power-hungry politician. And one with very little in the way of ethics or morals. But her mother was not the same as her father, and neither was Zadie like her father, even though the world out there wanted desperately to paint both women with the same brush.

WHEN SHE WENT limp in his arms, Zack looked down to find her unconscious. Swearing softly under his breath, he picked up the pace, racing toward his destination.

Thankfully he was decent at navigation in the dark. He'd taken a good long look along the way as they traveled here, once the arrangements had been made. But even now he was more and more concerned about Zadie. He shifted his grip on her legs and felt something sticky under his fingers. Now he had something else to worry about. She'd probably been cut on that broken window. If she was bleeding or bleeding badly, she probably wouldn't have noticed with their mad panic run to escape her captors. And, since he'd been carrying her, they had no light to notice anything amiss on her. Would she not have felt something? Should he slow or stop to investigate when he neared the rendezvous point with Bonaparte?

Up ahead, Zack could see the shape of a vehicle. He judged the outline, realized it would be Bonaparte's, and headed toward it. The light flashed once and then twice. As Zack neared it, he waved at the driver. And he kept on waving, making it look like something was wrong.

Finally the message came across, and Bonaparte hopped from the vehicle and raced toward him. He was only ten feet away when he reached him.

"Problems?" he asked in a low voice.

"Check her legs for me," he said. "She passed out while I was carrying her."

Immediately Bonaparte pulled up his phone, turned on the flashlight app, and checked. Indeed, a long gash with a steady flow of blood poured down her leg. Both of the men swore.

"We've got to get that stopped," Zack said, immediately heading to the vehicle, slipping her into the back seat, then finding and pouring out a bag that he searched through. Coming back with clean socks, he quickly made a tourniquet around the top of her leg and folded a strip of gauze into a pad to put pressure on the wound. With that done, he tied it up with another piece of gauze that he grabbed.

Awkwardly holding her in his lap, he got into the back seat and said to Bonaparte, "Drive quickly and carefully."

"I can be fast, or I can be careful," he said. "But being careful and fast, that's a different story."

"We have to get out of here," he said, "and we don't want to kill her in the process."

"Understood, but that'll need stitches."

"I'm hoping we can get some pressure on it to slow down the bleeding," he said. "It's bleeding way too fast."

"I know. I saw that. Anyway, we are on the road. Let's keep to the schedule, and I'll see what I can come up with."

"I'll stretch her out on the seat back here and see if I can work on that leg a bit more," he said. He shuffled over, laying her on the back seat, so her legs were on his lap. He kept the pressure on her bandage as he mopped up the blood coming from her leg. Now that most of the blood was gone, he took a better look under the gauze. It was hard to see, but he had his phone flashlight to give him a little bit of light. "A piece of glass is in her leg."

"Well, that's got to come out," Bonaparte said.

Zack nodded. "I know we probably shouldn't stop but at least tell me when we get to a good long stretch of road with no turns or potholes or dips in the road or whatever, so I can do a bit of surgery here." He fished into the back of his wallet; he had a couple tools in there, but it wasn't like he had tweezers. With his phone's flashlight and the vehicle's interior light, it wouldn't be enough. Yet this embedded glass was why he couldn't apply too much pressure to the wound, or it would just cut her deeper.

"Are we good for a while?" Zack asked Bonaparte.

"I can give you like four minutes, starting now."

Zack had a little lockpick set, and, using that, he carefully dug underneath the glass and popped it to the surface. He pulled it out and immediately clamped down tight on the wound with more gauze. "I got out the glass piece," he said, "but I can't be sure more isn't in there. If it's all out," he said, "the bleeding should slow down, unless something vital has been hit."

"Not in that location," Bonaparte said, "unless she's got a second injury." A few minutes later, Bonaparte called back, "Is it easing?"

"I hate to lift my hand and check," he said.

"If you got any water handy, keep that bandage moist. You don't want it to stick to her leg and dry out."

"And, if I leave it moist, we will have blood everywhere," he said.

"I know. I hear you. But you need to clean the wound anyway."

He pulled out one of the bottles of water in Bonaparte's bag, popped open the little cork with his teeth, and lifted the gauze slightly to look. He poured water around the wound to clean it as best as he could, then clamped down again with pressure, using a clean T-shirt from Bonaparte's bag. Zack mopped up the rest of her leg and washed it down as much as he could. She had pants on, but the glass had cut a long strip open. He noted she had a slight scratch as it got deeper and deeper to where her skin had been gashed open, so she must have put her weight on the broken glass as she went through the window.

Why didn't she say something? She had said she was cold. Maybe her sense of touch was numbed? She was probably too panicked and maybe even in shock to notice her injury until she couldn't keep up. He should have checked her sooner. He swore to himself for his oversight. "I shouldn't have let her run as much as she did," he said. "She's lost a lot of blood."

"She's young and healthy," Bonaparte said. "She will bounce back."

"True enough. It's just frustrating," he murmured. He looked down at the sleeping woman to see the waxiness on her skin. Her tummy was also concave, as if she hadn't had anything to eat in quite a while. He frowned at that. "Do we have any food in here?"

"I have a couple protein bars but nothing else."

"Depending on how long 'til our destination, she'll need food when she wakes up. They starved her in there."

"Bastards," he said in an aggravated tone.

"Left her for days without any kind of heat or blankets, until today," Zack said quietly. "She said the freezing was one of the biggest problems when she caught a chill. She couldn't get warm again."

"Is she well-dressed now?"

"No," he said, noting her feet were covered in socks, and that was it. "She also has no footwear." He studied her and swore softly and fluently. "Jesus, I should have picked her up right from the beginning. She would have done much better that way."

"But how could you know?" Bonaparte asked. "You can't blame yourself now. We got her away from there. We fixed the leg, and it's all good. Job accomplished."

"I wonder about that," he said.

"I have to get gas," Bonaparte said. "We are crossing the border as soon as we can, heading toward Greece. I believe Komotini is the closest big city there."

"ETA?"

"We're looking at 222 miles, so three hours for a normal driver."

"Well, with you driving, it will be faster."

"Definitely," he said. "And, once we get on the road in Greece, we'll stop and pick up some food somewhere."

"Good enough," he said. "I'll update Levi." Using his free forearm, he gently kept pressure on the wound as he texted Levi. **Zadie is free, in our vehicle heading toward Greece, not out of Turkey yet.**

A text came back. **Do you want a flight?**

He thought about that and responded, **Passport?**

It would take at least one day to get paperwork, Levi texted back. **Two days, most likely.**

Zack looked at Bonaparte. "Levi is asking about a flight."

"If we had the paperwork for her already, we could," he said, "but it won't come that fast."

"True enough. We can get a small private plane and make it, but we'd still likely be in trouble if we can't get out of this country first."

"I suggest we hit Greece first," he said, "where we can get her leg checked over and then make plans from that safety point."

Zack quickly passed that on to Levi.

Levi responded with, **Good enough.**

At that, Zack added, **Apparently Zadie's captors were a separate faction, two brothers and a wife, at the same place where the parents are being held under guard by the current regime. The trio are trying to get the brothers' father out of jail. Somehow they thought Zadie would give them leverage.**

Why would they care?

I don't know.

I'll do some research, Levi said.

When his phone rang, Zack answered it. "We could have done this from the beginning," he said humorously.

"Maybe we should have. How bad is she?"

"Bleeding pretty badly, but I've slowed it down."

"And yet you'll wait until you get to Greece?"

"The cuts are deep," he said, "but we want to get out of Turkey for sure. If we can find a place to stop and do some basic surgery, we'd do that too. Otherwise we need a clinic somewhere."

"Just across the border there's a small Greek village," he said. "A medical center is about a mile in. The doctor there is an expert, and he can fix her up."

"Now that would be perfect. Have you got us on satellite?"

"Yes, you're about ninety minutes out."

Zack had his phone on Speaker at that point.

Bonaparte laughed and said, "We'll make it in sixty."

Levi swore at him on the other side. "Bonaparte, safety first."

"Always." But immediately the car surged forward much faster.

"Well, we will either make it in sixty minutes," Zack said, hanging on to Zadie, "or we'll be dead."

"Check in either way," Levi said.

Just as Levi was about to hang up, Zack called out, "Wait. What's the doctor's name?"

"Passmore. Henry Passmore."

And, with that, there was nothing but a *click* on the phone. "We'll go see Dr. Henry Passmore."

"I heard. Keep her alive until then."

In fact, fifty-six minutes later, Bonaparte called out as he pulled off into the little village. Zack just shook his head. "Jesus Christ, you drove like a madman."

"But in control," he said. "Speed is good, but it's only good if you are in control."

"If you say so," he said.

They drove through the small town, and now just enough light was on the horizon, and Zack guessed it had to be around five or six in the morning. "The doctor won't even be at the clinic yet," he said.

"Tell Levi to contact him."

"I'm already doing that," he said. He sent a text to Levi. **We're here. How do we find the doctor? It's hardly waiting room hours.**

Go to the clinic. He's waiting for you.

He smiled at that. "Apparently the doctor is waiting for us," he said. He looked up the street. "Go forward two more blocks, then take a left."

Bonaparte followed his directions past several more corners; then he pulled into a small building with a little parking lot in the front. A light was on inside. As soon as he pulled up, Zack opened his passenger's door, gently slid her into his lap with her feet out the door first and struggled to get her outside the vehicle.

Once parked there, Bonaparte shut his door and asked, "Do you want me to carry her?"

Zack shook his head. "There's nothing to her."

They walked toward the clinic, when the side door opened, and a man in a white coat stood there. "I'm looking for Zack and Bonaparte," he said.

"We are looking for Henry Passmore."

The other man nodded agreeably. "You've found him. And this is the young lady with the leg wound?"

"Yes," they said.

He held the door open wider, "Bring her straight into one of my exam rooms."

They carried her through a series of rooms and finally to

a bed, where Zack laid her on top. The doctor bustled around, turning lights on, bringing over a tray with instruments. He immediately cut away the lower part of her pant leg and asked, "How did she get this?"

"Crawling out of a basement window where she'd been imprisoned for days by several men," Zack said bluntly.

The doctor shot him a look, shook his head, and said, "Levi mentioned something about a rescue."

"Yes, exactly. She didn't tell me that she was injured though. I pulled a piece of glass out of the wound on the way here, but I'm not sure if there isn't more." He was happy to see the bleeding had slowed, but it still moved sluggishly down her leg.

"After all this time, with the blood attempting to flush out all the foreign matter, something else is in there," the doc said. He brushed the men back and said, "Give me space." He sat down and got to work. He pulled another tiny piece of glass out with the help of his magnifying glass and tweezers and said, "That looks clean now." He quickly cleaned it up with an antibiotic solution, which made the blood run even more. "Looks like it just nipped a little bit of an artery here but not a real tear, just something struggling to heal."

"Will it heal?"

"Oh, yes," he said. "Absolutely. I'll have to stitch this closed." He immediately pulled over tools and sutures and got to work.

By the time he was done, Zack was leaning against the doorway, more relieved than he could say that somebody with his skill level had been here to patch her up.

The doctor stood. "It will leave a little bit of a scar but not too much of one."

Zack smiled as he looked down at the woman he'd helped out of the house. It was the first time that he had a chance to see her. She had high cheekbones, and her skin, although waxy pale, had a bit of a red flush coming back. She had a shock of golden reddish-brown hair, and she was lean, as in all-over lean. He frowned at that. "She looks as if she's been starved for weeks."

The doctor looked at her, shrugged, and said, "She's skinny, but that's the style for so many young women these days." He patted his own generous belly. "Not my style at all." He quickly bandaged up the leg wound, and, when he taped the gauze over top, he continued, "She needs antibiotics, and she needs pain meds, not to mention some rest."

"Any reason she can't travel?"

"No," he said. "She'll need the stitches in for a good ten, twelve days. Get her to a doctor afterward to take them out."

"Good enough."

"But the antibiotics should stop any infections," he said, "because you don't know what else might have gone in there with that glass." He walked over to his cabinets, using his key, opened up several of them, and pulled out bottles as he checked the labels. Then he walked over, grabbed a little pill bottle, and poured a bunch of capsules into his palm, counted out what he wanted. He put them in the bottle, popped the lid on it, wrote something on the blank white label, and handed it to him. "She needs four of these a day, preferably with food. They are likely to upset her stomach."

"Will do."

He walked toward different cabinets, pulled out a bottle of pain meds, and tossed it to him. "She can take up to four of these a day."

"Also good enough," he said. "How much do I owe

you?"

"Levi's already cleared the bill," Henry said. "He cleared it a long time ago. I've been looking for a chance to repay him, and this is the perfect opportunity."

"In that case," Bonaparte said with a smile, "thank you very much."

Just then came a murmur from the bed. Zack walked over, picked up Zadie's hand. "Take it easy," he said. "You collapsed, and we got you to a doctor right now."

Her eyes opened, and she withdrew from him, but he held her hand gently and said, "It's okay," he murmured. "Just take it easy."

She settled back into the exam table, her eyes wary as she studied his face, and he realized that she had yet to see who he was.

He gave her a big grin. "I'm the guy who helped rescue you from the basement. My name is Zack."

She studied him for a long moment; then he saw her visibly relax.

"I'm Zadie," she said, "and thank you for the rescue."

Chapter 4

Z ADIE'S GAZE ROAMED the stranger's face in front of her. Although she'd seen bits and pieces of him earlier, she never could get a good look at who he was. Short cropped dark, dark black hair, thick eyebrows, but a strong friendly face, square chin, and a thick, heavy build. The man beside him was a monster of a man. And then there was a guy in a white jacket.

She propped herself up on one elbow and cried out, "Good Lord." She looked at her leg. "What happened?"

"When you went through that basement window," Zack said, "you were cut up, and a couple pieces of glass ended up in your leg. I gather you didn't know about it because you said nothing?"

She looked at him in surprise, looked at her leg, and shrugged. "I'm sure I didn't know. I was pretty pissed I couldn't keep up with you though," she said. "Now I know why." She looked at the two men beside Zack and said, "If you had anything to do with my rescue and fixing me up, I thank you."

Bonaparte stepped forward, flashed her a smile, and bowed. "I'm Bonaparte, his partner."

She smiled up at him. "And I'm grateful. Thank you." She turned toward the doctor. "Are you the one who took care of my leg?"

Henry nodded in that genial manner of his. "I am. I've given these guys antibiotics and painkillers for you."

"I don't suppose I can have one or two of those right now?" she asked. "Even sitting up feels like somebody is cutting me apart."

"Well, somebody did," he said, as he walked over to grab a glass of water from the sink in one of those paper cups and came back, two pills in his hands. "Take these."

She tried to sit up a bit more but was at an awkward angle because they had propped up her leg on pillows.

Zack immediately grabbed her from behind by the armpits, propped her up, and sat her so she could lean against him. His manner had been a little rough, but she appreciated it because it worked. She tossed back the pills, swallowed them down, and handed the cup off to the doctor. "Thank you."

"You should start feeling better in about twenty minutes," he said.

She nodded, looking at her leg. "Where are we going from here?" she asked. "And where is here?"

"Greece," Henry said. "Just inside the border."

He gave the name of the village, but it wasn't one she knew. She nodded slowly. "So we are out of Turkey?" At Zack's nod, she leaned back against him and closed her eyes. "I'm damn grateful for that."

"What we don't have," Bonaparte said, "is your paperwork."

Her eyes flew open, and she studied the big man, who crossed his arms and widened his stance as he looked at her. "It's all back at the house where I was held," she said. "I just have my cell phone." She immediately patted her pants pockets. "My phone, where is my phone?"

"Where was it last?" Zack asked.

"Inside my pants leg," she said. "Honestly." She immediately checked her other leg and then crowed. "Look!" It was tucked inside the sock around the heavy cuff where it'd been rolled down. She pulled it out and held it up. "Now this I'm grateful to have."

"Does it have your documentation?"

"Well, it has photos," she said, turning it on, and then frowned. "But the battery is almost gone."

"That's to be expected. We'll charge it for you when we get back in the vehicle."

"And it does have my documentation in a sense, as I've got copies of my passport, my IDs. But that won't let me pass through any customs."

"No." The doctor smiled. "Now, if you want to go to Komotini, I might know somebody there who can help you."

She looked at him in surprise and then frowned. "In Komotini? I probably could go to the consulate and get some help too."

All the men nodded.

"That would be good if I could ask for a lift from here." She frowned, glanced around at the men in the clinic. "Nobody followed us, right?"

"No," Bonaparte said.

Zack joked, "Not unless they were flying a plane."

She looked at him in confusion.

"You have no idea how fast Bonaparte drives," he explained. "Nobody could have kept up."

"Okay," she said. "But what if they have some intel or just guessed at our closest safe border?"

"Do you really think those two brothers had that kind of

capability?"

She frowned at that, shook her head, and said, "No, I don't think so. What I don't understand is why they thought I would be a good choice for a prisoner exchange in the first place."

"I don't think they thought it through," Zack said. "Sounds like it was an opportunity they couldn't pass up. They might have decided that, finding you gone, it was not worth tracking you down anyway."

"Good," she said. "I'd like to get the hell out of here."

"I hear you," Zack said. "As soon as the doctor is ready to let you get up and walk around, just to make sure you're okay."

The doctor smiled and said, "You can leave anytime."

She slowly swung her leg off the raised pillow and shifted so she sat upright. As the leg came down, swinging a little more than she had expected, she shuddered, feeling the pain up and down her body. "We can leave now," she said gamely.

Bonaparte snorted. "Well, good to know you are ready, but we'd give you another few minutes until the painkillers kick in."

"I'd appreciate that," she said with a brave smile, "but I don't know if we have time." Just then her phone buzzed. She stared at it in surprise.

"Put it on Speakerphone," Zack said.

She nodded, answered it, saying, "Mom, is that you?"

Her mother's panicked voice cried out in relief. "There you are! We've been so worried."

"Why are you calling me right now?" she asked, rubbing her temple. She didn't know what to say to her mother. She glanced up; both of the men just shook their heads, and she frowned at them.

"I've been so worried," her mother said. "You never came back from your walk."

Zadie winced at that. "I'm so sorry," she said.

"Several days later I heard you were kidnapped. But you escaped, right?" her mom said evenly.

At that, she looked at the two men, shrugged, and replied, "Yes, I escaped."

"Well, thank God for that," she said. "I was so worried that something else might have happened to you. The least you could have done was let us know you were safe."

"I wasn't sure if they were tracking my phone calls or not," she lied.

"They probably are," her mother said with a sniff. "Especially now."

"Why now?"

"Your father isn't doing well."

"How bad is it?" she asked in alarm.

"It's his heart. But we're stuck here, and he won't make an issue of it, and no one is listening anyway. I've contacted a few people from our old life, and all they've said is that the media is silent. Only that we're guests of the government until their investigation is over. And you know how that will end. Still you got out, and, for that, I'm so happy," her mother said warmly.

"We'll get you out too," Zadie said, looking at the two men who rescued her.

"Not an issue right now. We're safe. I'm busy taking care of some personal stuff while I can," her mother said, her voice lowered to a whisper. "I want to make sure you're okay. I don't know how long before they find out what I'm doing, so I have to be careful."

"Mom, forget about me. I'm fine. Let's just keep you safe, and we're coming to get you."

"No," her mother said firmly. "I know I'd hoped I could leave with you, but, when they wouldn't let you leave, then you were kidnapped, … well, it's not likely to happen now."

Zadie didn't know what to do.

"I can't talk long. I'll call you again." And, with that, her mother hung up.

Zadie stared at her phone, then slowly placed it in her lap. "She hung up."

"She sounded well though," Zack said quietly. "Fairly calm. Unhurt. Although I'm sorry about your father's condition."

"I forgot about his heart condition," she murmured. "I've been so focused on convincing my mother to get out, knowing there was no way to help him. He'd prefer to die before they make a circus show with him as the central character." Just then her stomach growled. She sighed. "So I don't suppose you have any food in the main part of the village, do you? Restaurants? Cafés? Grocery stores?" She looked at the paper cup supply. "Or more water?"

The doctor smiled. "The water I can do something about, but I'm not so sure about food—it's too early, even for our little village."

She nodded and groaned. "I can survive a little bit longer." When he returned with a much larger glass of water, she drank it back and smiled. "That feels much better," she said. Using Zack's shoulder, she hopped up onto her good leg and gingerly put some weight on the sore one. She caught her breath and held it, while she experimented with hobbling around. "Painful," she admitted. "And as long as we don't have to run for our lives again," she said with a side look at

Zack, "I should be fine, particularly if I get to lie in the back seat of a car with my leg propped up."

"That's how I suggest you travel," the doc said. "The leg needs to be up to help take the pressure off."

She nodded. It didn't take much longer to get everybody out to the vehicle, and her leg propped up in the back, the doctor donating a pillow for her. Along with Bonaparte's bag as a pillow for her head, she was relatively comfortable. She thanked the doc again. He just smiled, nodded, and headed back, closing the clinic door behind him. "I presume he will lock that, right?"

"Absolutely," Zack said, as he got into the front seat. He turned to look at her. "So not any food here, but we can stop at a restaurant up ahead."

"Maybe," she said. "Maybe I should just try to sleep."

"If you're tired, do so," he said. "We are a good couple hours outside of Komotini."

"Absolutely." Just then her phone rang again. "Uh-oh, it's Mom again. What's up, Mom?" She again put her phone on Speaker.

"Help," her mother called through the phone frantically. "Help. I think he's dead. Now they want something from me. ... Hel—" And, just like that, the phone went dead.

Zadie bolted upright. "Oh, my God." Her gaze went from her phone, like a bomb about to go off, then stared at the two men in shock. "What the hell?"

They looked at each other, then at her. "Oh no," they said. "You're not going back there."

She stared at them in shock. "What do you mean, I'm not going back there? This is my mother. She's obviously in a crisis. Of course I'm going back there. Besides, you got me out of there, so you can get her out." She stopped. "In truth,

I should never have left without her." She closed her eyes, overcome with guilt, repeating, "I should never have left without her."

"What are you talking about? We rescued you, and you were in no condition to tell us that your mother needed rescuing too."

"All this happened so fast," she said. "And my mother's situation just now escalated for sure. But I did hear the house guards talking about how they would move my parents. Somebody laughed in the background, saying, *Yeah, six feet under.* And then I was attacked."

"What do you mean, you heard them?"

"The regular guards were standing outside. I went out to check on them, to see the timing of their rounds, and they were standing outside, talking. I was on the other side of the trees. I walked past them, and they separated off, and someone jumped me."

"Maybe you were jumped because you heard them," he said.

"I don't know," she said, shaking her head. "The normal guards are separate from my jailers. But regardless, my mother, she is not part of this. Please, we can't just leave her there. You got here in what, an hour, two hours? Rather than going to Komotini, let's go back and grab her."

"You don't know what happened to her," Bonaparte said carefully. "That sounded like somebody very panicked."

"You think?" she cried out, her voice rising. "Please, don't make me walk away from my mother like this."

The two men looked at each other. Bonaparte shrugged and said, "Well, I'm up for it." He pulled off to the shoulder, then turned back in the direction they'd come from. Within seconds he was flying at top speed again. If he had his way, she just knew he'd push the speed even faster if she didn't protest. But she'd start screaming soon.

"Tell us everything you know," Zack said, twisting in his seat so he could look at her. "And if you know anything about where they were taking your parents. I know what you said earlier, but anything else you can remember will help."

"No, nothing other than that. I hardly got a chance to visit with my parents. When I arrived, the house guards were very clear that I wasn't leaving, and I threw a fit. So did my mother. My father just ignored me. As soon as I heard that, I made plans for at least me to escape and get more help and come back for my mother. I was just locking down those plans when I was snatched up and somehow squirreled into the damn basement without realizing where I was for sure," she said. "While there, I had no idea what was going on with my parents. I had no contact with her until she called me these two times this morning."

"So we don't know that your parents are still at the same house where we rescued you. Which is a pretty big assumption," Zack warned. "We don't know what is going on with your parents even now. They were imprisoned by the new government, but, for all you know, the ones who kidnapped you were part of your parents' imprisonment team."

"The guards were always laughing," she said sadly. "And I know the government is just enough up in arms right now about my father that anything could happen."

"And your mother had nothing to do with your father's activities?"

"No," she said, shaking her head vehemently. "She never did. I know people blamed her because she was always in the background, but it's not as if she could have stopped him at any time."

"Possibly not," Zack said, "but many people would have blamed her anyway."

"Exactly." She worried, just having heard her mom's voice. She quickly redialed, but there was no answer. "Oh, my God," she said, her voice barely audible. "What if it's already too late?"

"Then we'll find out soon," Bonaparte said.

"How soon?"

"I'll see if I can beat my record," he said.

She was sorry she had asked because, all of a sudden, it was as if the entire vehicle was flying through the air. She gasped as she looked at his speedometer, but it was off the dial. "How can you possibly drive this fast?" she asked, staring in amazement.

Zack twisted, looked at her, and said, "You might as well lie down and rest. Think about anything you can that might help us."

"Okay," she said.

"If they were to take your parents somewhere, where would they take them? And, if they weren't moving them, would they kill them right now? Is there any reason to keep them alive?"

"I don't know," she said.

Zack looked at her gently. "You know more than you think," he said. "So spend the next few minutes lying there, thinking about it."

She collapsed back down and stared at the roof of the car. "Dear God," she said. "If I had known she was in immediate danger, I would never have left without her. You know that, right?"

"I know," he said, "but we came in to rescue you, and that was our mission."

"Oh, my God," she said, "I didn't even think about her."

"Stop it," he said. "You couldn't have changed it. We are the ones who left without her."

"I know. I know. I know," she said, crying out. Sinking back, she crossed her arms over her chest and laid down. The vehicle shot through the air faster than any she'd ever been in before. "Dear God," she whispered, "let me please be in time."

ZACK SETTLED INTO his seat and looked at Bonaparte. "This isn't exactly part of the plan," he said softly.

"Plans change," Bonaparte said.

"I get it," he said. "I better update Levi." He brought out his phone, and, instead of explaining it all in a text, he called him. As soon as Levi answered, he quickly explained the sudden turn of events.

"Did you consider that it might be a trap?"

"I'm not sure that it would matter," he said. "The fact of the matter is that Zadie is concerned that her mother is an innocent party and wants us to save her."

"And what about getting Zadie away safely?"

"Well, we did that," he said, a note of humor in his voice. "But the trouble is, she insists on going back."

"Of course she does," Levi said. "I'll call you back after we check out some satellite feeds."

Zack ended the call and turned to check on her. Her eyes were closed, and he didn't want to disturb her. In a low tone, he updated Bonaparte. "With satellite, they might see if anybody has been removed from the place."

"Is that good or bad if they have though?" he asked.

"Not sure it makes any difference anyway," Bonaparte said, his eyes on the roadway.

"I know," Zack said, frowning. "And maybe they are blaming the parents for the daughter escaping. That would make more sense to me."

"Yes, that could be it," Bonaparte said with a nod. "Maybe they were punishing them."

"It's possible," he said. "Interesting that the mother managed to call to let out a warning."

"She probably still had the phone in her hand from calling her daughter a few minutes earlier. There wasn't any reason to be too worried about her after the first call, but she's definitely in more trouble now after the second call."

"Yeah, I heard her scream," Zack said grimly. "Nothing nice about that sound." As a matter of fact, it brought back all kinds of horrible notions. And, if there was ever any soft spot in the world, it was the fate of everyone's mothers. He shifted the seat backward and said, "I'll catch five."

"Sure," Bonaparte said. "I'll just sail back the way we came." He started whistling. "Hopefully by the time we get close, they'll have satellite feed again. We need to know if any vehicles left, and we need to get back into that house."

"Great," he said. "I went through a hell of a lot to get her out of there. I'm not looking forward to going back in."

"Well, think of it this way," Bonaparte said with a laugh. "This time, we are likely to go through the front door, instead of creeping in through a window, like a robber in the night."

"The trouble with the front door," he said, "is someone with a weapon will likely be waiting for us."

"Bring them on," Bonaparte said. "I'm ready for a good dustup. How about you?"

Chapter 5

ZADIE HEARD THE guys' conversation in the front seat and realized that it was typical of others. It wasn't their mother in trouble right now. Zadie knew her mother was a hard sell to leave her father, so Zadie figured she'd had to free herself, then come back with reinforcements to free her mother. If only her mother had been cooperative from the first. But that had never been part of Zadie's original plan. When she had been setting up her ultimate escape plan, it had hopefully been for the two of them. She had planned to take her mother back to America and to live quietly.

As for her father, she knew no hope remained there. He was doomed to die in Istanbul. And, while her mother would never leave him willingly, Zadie had hoped she could convince her mother that it was the right thing to do with all the added unrest in Turkey. Now all Zadie could do was hope they made it there in time.

Somewhere along the drive, she must have dozed off. When she woke up, they were still traveling at an astronomical speed. Zadie realized she should be grateful she was even alive, considering how fast they were traveling. Although the driver appeared completely confident, she wasn't. Zadie had traveled the world in various forms, but this was the closest to flying without actually getting off the ground that she'd ever experienced. Still, the movement helped her drift back asleep. When she woke again, she heard Zack's voice.

"We've got satellite feeds! According to Levi, no vehicle has left the premises."

"Good," he said. "Then they are still in the house."

"If that's a good thing," Zack said. "That means they might have fortressed in."

"Only if they are expecting an attack. For all we know, they've already snuck out some other way with no vehicles, like we did."

"I wondered about that, but then they had to be expecting satellite feeds to capture those movements."

"Who all has satellite?" she asked, smothering a yawn.

"Way too many people," Zack said, twisting to look at her. "How do you feel?"

"I'm starving," she said bluntly. "I know we are in a rush, and we need to get back to my mother. Is there any way to run through someplace and pick up food and carry on?"

"I'm not sure there is," he said.

Bonaparte said, "There is a protein bar in my bag, under your head, if you want to get that."

Immediately she struggled upright, dug through the bag, found the protein bar, and tore into it. The two men listened to her eat in silence. When she took the last bite, she remarked, "This tastes like sawdust, but I was running on empty."

"We will all be running on empty soon enough," Zack said. "We also haven't had much rest."

She winced at that. "I know, and I'm sorry," she said. "I was really looking forward to a room in Komotini, until I realized what was going on."

"I hear you. Your mother sounded completely different

in those two calls. Her first phone call raised no alarms or immediate red flags."

"I can only blame the pain, the drugs, and the circumstances for that. None of it connected until she screamed for help into my ear. Believe me. I feel terrible."

"No point in feeling terrible," he said. "Let's sort this out as much as possible. Why would somebody hurt her?"

"Getting rid of the evidence," she said bluntly. "My father, well, he will be on trial for his crimes. His conviction is almost guaranteed."

"So somebody will save the country the cost of a trial and just kill them both?"

"Maybe," she said. "So many political factions are going on in Turkey right now. It's just unbelievable how the country runs or survives."

"Is your father guilty?"

"Hell, yes," she said. "I've no sympathy for his fate. I just didn't want my mother mixed up in it."

"I know. Are you absolutely sure she's innocent?"

"You've asked that before," she said, noting his doubt, yet knowing everyone wondered the same thing.

"I know. You have to seriously answer that yourself," Zack said. "I don't know anything about the situation, but, like the rest of the public, when somebody stands by her man all those years, you have to wonder if she wasn't in the know about it."

"She was in the know for some of it," Zadie said. "Does that make her guilty?"

"Many people would say so, yes," he said.

"Even though he beat her?"

"Your father?" he asked in shock. He twisted to look at her, and she nodded.

"Yes," she said. "My mother was very much a battered woman. She was terrified to leave and terrified to stay. She's no more guilty of any of those crimes than I am."

"Good enough," he said. "The trouble is, not everybody will believe you."

"Nobody would believe me," she said, "but it is what it is, and I can't help that."

"Do you know how to get to where they were in that house?"

"Their bedrooms were up the stairs, on the back right," she said. "Second bedroom after you turned a quarter at the top of the stairs."

"Locks in the door?"

"No," she said. "Bars on the window."

"Bars in the downstairs windows?" Zack asked, frowning.

"I saw them in the basement and on the upper floor where the bedroom windows are, but not on the main floor," she said, "but definitely steel bars are involved."

"So it's a prison for sure."

"They also have guards."

"How many guards, and how heavily armed?"

"Four guards, with handguns," she said. "No rifles but that doesn't mean they didn't have them somewhere."

"Any other men come and go?"

"Not while I was there," she said. "Not that I saw."

"And the two men who imprisoned you?"

"They worked at the house. The woman was one of the cooks." She brought up the images she had on her phone. "I took these in case that helps. It's hard to describe people afterward, whereas a picture is worth one thousand words."

"One of the cooks?" He turned to look at the photo she

held up.

"The house came with its own staff. So the main cook and an assistant cook, a housekeeper, and somebody who cleaned up around the place," she said with a shrug, as she thought about it. "For all I know, they were all hired gunmen too."

"The woman you spoke with while you were jailed, she was the assistant cook in the kitchen?"

"Yes," she said. "I did see her up and around some of the bedrooms too."

"It was a great disguise too," Zack said. "Very few people actually recognize 'the help.' It's a sad fact."

"Anything else you can tell us?" Bonaparte asked.

"No," she said. "I didn't even realize I was seriously in danger. They told me that I wasn't allowed to leave, but it was a flat-out 'don't even expect to be leaving' kind of a comment. I did talk to my parents, and my father wanted me to leave too, but he couldn't arrange for it because the guards there refused."

"But you made arrangements yourself?"

"Well, I was putting final touches into place, yes," she said. "I was literally setting up my last steps when I heard them talking outside about killing my parents."

"Are other people expecting you anywhere right now?"

"I told a few people I was visiting my parents and would try to get away—friends, colleagues, that kind of a thing. But nobody had dates yet because I didn't know how fast I could leave the country. But I was supposed to let them know when I was free and clear."

"And, since you woke up, have you contacted anyone?"

"No," she said shortly. "Apparently I'm not thinking too clearly yet."

"That leg injury is nothing to trifle with," Zack said in a soothing voice. "The drugs that you were under while in the prison didn't help, and now you've got painkillers and antibiotics in your system. If we are lucky, you won't have an allergic reaction between the drugs."

"I don't know what they gave me, "she said, "but it's possible that they would drug my parents if they're moving them."

"That would make sense," he said, "but why move them?"

"To get rid of them?" she asked.

"Then drugs aren't needed. Just a bullet would do."

ZACK KNEW HE shouldn't have said that, but it slipped out. At her startled gasp, he turned and whispered, "Sorry."

She shook her head and stared at him, her eyes big globes of pain. "I feel so shitty," she said. "I should have insisted we get her right from the beginning. I wasn't thinking clearly at the time you found me and rescued me."

"Don't let it bother you. Remember. You didn't have a choice in the matter. We were focused on getting you out of there. We didn't realize your mother was in so much danger at that time."

"How much longer?"

He checked his watch and said, "About forty-five minutes."

"I'd like to lay down and sleep again," she said, "but my mind is churning."

"Your leg can't heal without sleep, and you can't do any running around while we are out there either," he said. "You need to prepare yourself for staying in the vehicle the entire time."

She glared at him.

He shook his head. "No," he said. "If I go in there looking for your mother, I can't be watching and helping you get in and out too. Trust me that I can get her out—if she is there, if she is alive, if she is mobile. The same as I got you out."

"She can't crawl out a window and go through broken glass," she warned.

"Well, I was hoping to miss that part this time," he said with a smile. "But we'd have to improvise because we don't have a plan in place. We also may have to take out four, if not six or seven people," he reminded her. "And that won't be an easy walk in the park either."

"The guards have taken over two rooms on the main floor. When you go in the front door, they're on the right side. There's a hallway, and several rooms along there the guards took over for their quarters. They have offices, computers, monitors, camera equipment in there. And then a couple rooms with bunks."

"So all the guards are on the main floor?"

She nodded. "Yes."

"Any idea approximately how many rooms are in the house?"

"Possibly sixteen or seventeen," she said, "but I don't know what's in the basement. It was completely black."

"Prison cells probably," he said. "Don't know if there was anything else because I didn't get a chance to check it out myself. More rooms, similar in size, and not all the windows had bars," he said.

"No?" she said. "That's surprising. Mine did."

"No," he said, "not the bigger ones. Maybe they were

used for something else. So maybe the small rooms had those little windows with bars, like you were talking about in your cell."

"I have no clue," she said, as she sagged against the back seat again. "I just wish this was over with, and I wish my mother was in this vehicle with us, safe."

Zack twisted back around, slid a look at Bonaparte. The two men exchanged hard glances because, when it came to a change of plans like this, things tended to go very wrong. They were safe and clear, but now, going back for her mother—an emotional decision—was not a smart business decision, and Zack somehow didn't think it would go anywhere near as smoothly as Zadie was hoping for. As a matter of fact, he didn't think it would go smoothly at all.

Chapter 6

HUDDLED IN THE back seat, her leg as elevated as she could get it, Zadie waited in the darkness. They'd arrived twenty minutes ago, and every minute seemed interminable for her. She thought the wait to get here had been bad on the drive, but, with Bonaparte driving like a crazy man, she'd been half wondering if she'd even arrive alive. Now all she could think about was her poor mother.

The men had given her a strict order, staying where she was, and, given the state of her leg, it wasn't too hard to follow. But it was painfully difficult to wait and to worry. Despite the time of day—afternoon—the dark cloud cover blocked out the sun and allowed the men to proceed. Otherwise they would have waited for nightfall.

She kept looking at her phone constantly, checking for any messages, but there was nothing. Both men had her number, and of course so did her mother. Zadie had to trust that the men would get her mother out of there, the same as they had gotten Zadie out. Preferably in a much better way. So much was counting on what happened next, following her mother's frantic phone call. And Zadie didn't even want to think about the fact that maybe her mother was no longer alive. It would just cripple Zadie.

She knew many in the world blamed her mother for everything that had gone wrong in Turkey, the same as they had blamed her father. And Zadie also understood Zack's point, but, the thing was, her mother was really a simple woman. And she had loved her husband to distraction. She'd taken the abuse because he kept making excuses, saying it was okay, and he didn't really mean it.

Zadie had been trying to get her mother away from her father for a long time. And now, just when she was about to make that happen, somebody had kidnapped Zadie. It was incredibly frustrating. You set all these plans in motion, and then it didn't do you any good.

She laid back down, stared out through the window to the sky above for the umpteenth time, wondering what was going on inside. Part of her wondered if she should have just stayed in Komotini, where she was safe. If she was taken now, it'd be that much harder for her to escape. Her leg was killing her. She'd taken the antibiotics and another pain pill as soon as they arrived. She could only hope that, if she did have to move, the pain pill would kick in, and her leg would be strong enough for her to rely on. No guarantee though. The painkillers had taken the edge off but didn't really help with the strength to move her legs.

She needed to be curled up in bed for a few days to heal. Not curled up in the back seat of a car, parked in the middle of nowhere, hoping that the two men who had driven her here didn't get shot. And, if they were, then what was she supposed to do?

Just then her phone buzzed. She looked down to see a text from Zack, saying, **We are here.**

She smiled at that and sent back a thumbs-up. What else was she supposed to say? That they were there didn't mean it was all good. That they had arrived didn't mean that they would have a chance to do a full search of the place either.

Nor did it mean her mother was fine.

Zadie laid down and waited, the phone resting on her chest, in case she dozed off.

When there wasn't another text for ten minutes, she started counting the time. At fifteen, she frowned. How long would it take for them to make a plan? How long would it take them to find out who was inside and who wasn't? So many damn questions.

At twenty minutes, she marked off each successive minute in her mind. At twenty-five and then thirty, she fretted. By the time forty-five minutes had gone by, she was seriously getting worried.

And then she thought about all the things that took forty-five minutes to do in her world. That was everything from peeling a pot of potatoes and getting them fully cooked, to her normal morning walk that she liked to do when she wasn't into running. It took her forty-five minutes to do a lap around their property on a slow move. It really wasn't all that long, considering the two men had to scout out what was going on, find a way to get back in, potentially take out the guards, of which there may be more than they thought, find her mother, hopefully in some shape that she could be moved, and then they all had to get out.

It could take hours.

At that, she groaned and closed her eyes, determined to at least rest a bit.

The last thing she needed was to be so worked up that by the time they returned here that she'd be of no use to her mother because Zadie would be so exhausted.

Just when she determined that was the best avenue, headlights shone in the back of her vehicle. She sucked in her breath and swore silently. She didn't need anyone to come up and stop at the vehicle, asking who she was, what the hell she was doing here.

It came up slowly, then drove on past. She sat up between the two seats and watched as the vehicle carried on. It had gone so slow that she worried about it. Were they coming back to check on the car? Or was it somebody looking to steal the vehicle? She wanted to think it was some Good Samaritan worried about a car being broken down and wanting to offer help, but, more than likely, it was the exact opposite. Even worse would be if they called in the vehicle and said something suspicious was going on.

Bonaparte had pulled it off the shoulder and had parked it close to the trees. So there could be many reasons for it being here. It didn't look like it had crashed or had a flat tire, but who knew what people thought.

Slowly she laid back down, wondering if she should send the guys a text, letting them know. Exactly who were these people driving by? And how many vehicles would likely come upon her? Because she hadn't worked all that into her equation. There was always so much worry she could pass around before she couldn't handle too much more.

Just when she contemplated getting out of the vehicle to find a place in the woods to sit down and wait, her phone buzzed again. She checked her phone, but, as soon as she lifted it to look, the vehicle that had gone past was slowly coming back. She swore, grabbed her pillow, and checked to see if anything else was left inside the vehicle. The men had left it relatively clean, taking their bags with them, as they might need them, depending on what they came upon, and had left her a little water and her medications.

With the door opened slightly, she waited to make sure that she was out of their rearview as they came round the corner, and, taking one last look around the interior of the vehicle, she snuck out the side and slipped over to several trees.

Just trying to walk was damn-near killing her with pain. Giving her a hell of a good idea that she had very little reserve of strength there, if she needed to run. Which meant she had to hide first. She moved over a couple more trees and hid in the back behind several that were close together. If somebody came looking for her, it wouldn't be too hard to find her.

She had filled her pockets with as much as she could and held her phone up. If need be, she could tuck it into her bra. She looked at the trees, trying to find a place to hide. Climbing up was one option but not a good one. Continuing to travel wasn't ideal either.

She managed to get up into one tree with a low lying branch. But her leg wasn't making it easy. Holding back cries of pain, she got up another branch and then another one. She had to make sure she was above eye level and hidden from flashlights.

It took her another ten minutes to get there, and, by that time, the headlights were coming upon the car again. For a fleeting moment, she wondered if she was being a complete fool, but it slowed and rolled to a stop on the road across from Bonaparte's car. The last thing she wanted to do was end up without a set of wheels, but, even worse than that, she didn't want to get caught by somebody who would take her to the Turkish authorities.

She had no clue who was behind her original kidnapping—surely not the hired staff she recognized in the main house—so she had to be cautious. Pulling out her phone, she read Zack's message, which basically said, *No news yet.* She sent a quick text. **Vehicle stopped. Hidden in trees.**

Immediately he texted back, **Are you okay?**

She smiled, wrote, **Yes, they are searching the car.**

She could just imagine his response to that. She watched as two men got out, searched around and inside the vehicle, and then shone flashlights toward the trees. They walked around a little bit, using the flashlights to check for tracks. But the ground was dry, and there was no sign of her footprints. At no point in time did they look up.

She waited in the tree with bated breath, hoping like hell these guys would take off. And they did, but it took a while. Finally, with them taking several photographs of the vehicle, they got back into their car and left. As soon as they did, she immediately texted Zack. **They're leaving. But they searched the inside and took photographs of the license plate and the vehicle.**

Did you know them?

No, just two men, tall, in uniforms.

He immediately sent back one single word. **Shit.**

She gave a crack of sad laughter. That was one way to put it. She didn't know what she should do. Were they coming back yet again with a tow truck? Would the police come to check it out to see if it was stolen? And then she thought about it and texted him back, **Did you steal the vehicle?**

As she waited for him to get back to her, her reaction set in.

Swearing, she sat down on the closest branch and hugged the tree. She sent back a quick message. **You better get back here soon. I'm up the tree, and I'm not sure I can get down. For all I know, we've got cops coming to tow away the car.**

When she got a response from him, she was surprised.

Understood. But it really didn't tell her anything, Zack was a man of few words.

ZACK WAS ONCE again inside the basement of the house, haven gotten in the way he had gotten Zadie out. With Bonaparte at his side, they'd already done a full sweep of the basement, but it was empty. Now they were listening through vents to find out who was where. Counting the number of enemies inside.

Once they went up the stairs, it would be hard to keep their presence hidden. So far, they'd heard a couple men, but that was it. They needed to hear a lot more before they could make a clear-cut plan.

Zack couldn't believe that somebody came across the vehicle. There'd been few places to hide it, so they'd just pulled off the road, hoping it would be ignored. But obviously its presence caught someone's attention, and they had come and done a thorough search.

The thought of her up in a tree with her wounded leg sent ice through his veins. It would have been hard enough for her to get up, but trying to get her back down again without hurting her wouldn't happen. Not to mention they were inside the house, and they had no time to get her. Not until they were done here. Trouble was, there'd been no confirmation that her mother was even in the residence.

They had attached listening bugs in the vents, trying to hear part of the conversations on the first floor, but, so far, the guards had been arguing about beer and dinner. That two guards were here meant that there should be something worth guarding. But, other than that, there was no conversation about the prisoners under house arrest.

As he was about to pull off the three bugs from the vents, he heard someone on the stairs, coming down. He exchanged hard glances with Bonaparte, and both of them melted into the shadows. The guard walked down the stairs, turned the corner, and headed to the far corner. Zack and Bonaparte had already searched this floor. Rooms were back there, but they were empty. Zack thought he heard voices, and he had to wonder, had they missed a room? But the guard was talking to himself as he walked up and down the hallways and then headed to the stairs again.

"Complete waste of time this is," he snapped. "The basement is empty. Why go down and check?" he muttered.

But whoever had sent him down had better instincts than he did because both Bonaparte and Zack were here. But the guard didn't make any attempt to do a thorough search, or they would have been found.

He muttered a little bit more as he moved toward the stairs. Zack gathered that he felt he should be sitting back, watching the game, and having a beer. It was an interesting concept for a guard. Zack wondered if it was the same guard who had been involved in Zadie's kidnapping.

The woman who'd been involved in Zadie's kidnapping had had access to the rest of the house and could have let her accomplices in any number of times, so that trio could also have been involved in the parents' crimes, in the guards' activities for the current regime, and who knew what else. Or maybe not. If they could find the female kidnapper, that would be a different story. Zack would be happy to haul her away with him too. But she wouldn't go quietly, and his priority was the mother, not the assistant cook and maid.

With a final look at Bonaparte, the two men nodded and crept up the stairs. Since they were at the back of the house, opposite the front door, Zack tipped to the left, where the guards would be, while Bonaparte did a quick search on the right. Zack cleared one room and was heading up to the second one when he heard voices down at the far end, two doors down. He did a quick search of the second room, then made his way to the third. It was empty too.

Bonaparte joined Zack then, who held up his finger, connected in a circle to his thumb, saying zero, as in he hadn't found anybody else on the main floor. Which meant anybody here was in that final room.

Zack wondered for a moment if they could make it up the stairs. He motioned upstairs to Bonaparte, who frowned, looked in the direction of the guards, gave a shrug and a nod. And then, in a move Zack had never seen before from his partner, Bonaparte grabbed the railing right from where they stood, which was at least six feet up. He jumped, lightly landing on the banister, and was up and out of sight in seconds.

Zack quickly put away his gun and followed his partner. If they could search the upstairs, while the guards were in one room downstairs, that would be ideal.

Upstairs, they did a quick sweep from room to room to room, but nobody was here.

Back at the same location again, the two looked at each other and frowned. He pulled out his phone and sent a message to Zadie. **No sign of anyone but the guards in the one room.** Then he pocketed the phone and whispered to Bonaparte. "We've got no argument with the guards," he murmured.

Bonaparte nodded. "But they will know what happened to her mother. And we can't leave without that information."

Zack winced at that because Bonaparte was right. Zadie was persistent, and, although they could let her deal with the fact that they didn't question the guards after they came all this way, that wasn't something he was comfortable doing. He nodded and said, "Let's go get the guards then."

They made their way down the stairs by again walking along the top edge of the railing, until they got low enough to lightly jump and land softly with his feet widespread. They walked a little bit down the hallway, and Zack heard voices at the end. He raced forward with his gun out, Bonaparte on his heels. At the noise, the gunmen burst through the door of the room, and Zack held up a gun and said, "Halt."

Three men all froze to see the two of them there. Anger flashed across their faces and then calculating looks as they studied the weapons the two men had.

Zack immediately raised his gun a little higher and motioned at them to turn around and go back into the room.

They backed up slowly into the room.

At the doorway, Zack glanced around, but it was just a large office with several desk monitors. "Interesting. You chose a room well away from the action and without a back door in case there was a problem," he said.

Bonaparte nodded. "Bad choice of location."

The men just glared at them, letting them know that they understood English perfectly.

"What happened to the older couple who was here?" Zack asked menacingly. The men just gave him blank looks. He smiled, nodded, and said, "I will shoot you point-blank, and I won't give a shit." His tone was low, but his words rang true. "I want to know what happened to the old woman."

Instantly the men looked at each other. One man was about to give him a bit of a smart answer; Zack could see it coming with a curl of his lips. He popped him in the knee before he got the chance.

The man went down screaming. Zack kept the gun on him for a second, but then moved it between the two of them still standing. "I'll do it again," he said. "The mother who was here, the woman, what happened to her?"

The men shrugged. "Two men came and took her."

"And her husband?" Zack asked.

The man shook his head slowly.

"What would they do with her?"

"I don't know for sure," he said. "There is a chance that they would kill her. But they wanted something."

"Of course they did. What did they want?"

"Some books that her husband kept."

"And her husband, what happened to him?"

At that, he stilled and said, "He didn't make it."

"Right, so they killed the politician, and now the wife knows that she will die because there is no need to keep her alive. But they wanted something from her first?"

He nodded slowly.

"And what exactly is this book?"

"I don't know," he said. "They just said they wanted the book."

"Did she say she would get it for them?"

"Yes," he said.

"Where is it then?"

At that, he fell silent. Bonaparte immediately lifted his gun, pointed it at his knee.

He screamed out, "No, no, I think they would go to their house."

"What house?"

"Another one, the one they lived at most of the time."

"Did you have anything to do with kidnapping the daughter?" Zack asked.

"We did not kidnap her," the man protested. "No, she came here to visit her parents, and then was told she was a prisoner," he said.

The other gunman shrugged. "We had orders. She shouldn't have come."

"Maybe not," Zack said, "but she was kidnapped from here. Did you have anything to do with that?"

He frowned and looked at the others. Immediately they shook their heads. "No, we did not."

"Really?" he said. "Then what happened to her?"

They looked at each other, shrugged, and said, "We thought the same men took her."

"No, they didn't," Zack said with a sigh.

"Now I know you are dying to give me the address, where they took the old woman to," Bonaparte said, his voice harsh. When nobody answered, he took a step closer.

Immediately the one at the back said, "I don't know the address, but the daughter should have it."

"And yet she is missing, isn't she?"

"We know nothing about the daughter," said the one on the floor, as he gasped in pain. "She was here, and then she was gone."

"And you did nothing?"

"Of course we did something," he said in outrage. "We searched for her, but she was gone."

"She was being held in your basement," he said in a quiet voice. "Where is your hired help?"

He looked up at him. "The cook is gone, as well as her

husband and brother-in-law," he said. "When the daughter, the prisoner, left, and then after her father died, there was no need to keep the staff on."

"Where does the cook live?"

"In the village," he said, "not far from here."

"We need her contact information."

The men frowned as they looked around, and then the one supplied it willingly. "It is not far from here," he said. "You should find it easily."

"Did she work here alone?"

"Her brother did a lot of work outside. And when we needed extra help, he was supposed to be here, but he doesn't have any training."

"Understood," he said. "Now look after your comrade," Zack said. He and Bonaparte slowly backed out. "If you come after us," Zack said, "I have a bullet here for each of you."

"Not if we shoot you first," the third man snapped from the back.

Immediately Bonaparte fired and took out his gunhand. The man screamed as he clutched his arm against his chest. "Well, now you won't be shooting us, will you?" Bonaparte's voice was hard. "I'll take out your legs too if I think you're coming after us." And he immediately moved the gun over to the second man.

The second man held up his hands. "Go," he said. "We don't have any argument with you."

"Good enough," Bonaparte said. "But this is your only warning. If we see you again, it's a bullet between the eyes." And, like that, the two of them melted away.

Once in the trees, they stopped and waited to see if the guards would come after them. "What do you think?"

Bonaparte asked. "Are they smart enough to leave well enough alone?"

"I hope so for their sake," Zack whispered. "I don't think their paychecks are big enough to get killed."

"Good," he said. "Now let's get the hell back to that vehicle before we lose it."

Chapter 7

SOMEONE CALLED TO Zadie from down below. She froze in the tree. She hadn't heard anybody arrive. She gave her head a shake and looked around her. It was pitch-black, and she couldn't see anything.

Down below, the man called up softly, "Are you awake, Zadie?"

"Yes," she whispered, relieved to hear Zack's voice below her. Immediately she heard him clambering up the branches toward her. "Careful," she said. "They are not very thick."

"They'll be fine," he said, and suddenly he was here, standing on a branch, staring up at her only a foot below. "There you are. Come on. Let's go. We need to pick up the vehicle before somebody comes back and grabs it."

She nodded. "I was thinking of that," she said, "but ..." And she looked around nervously. "I'm more than a little worried about getting out of here."

"Which is why we will take care of it. I've picked a trail already. I want you to get on my back and hang on tight," he said.

"With just my arms? Because I can't get my legs around you."

"I know," he said. He turned, so she was behind him. "I want you to grab on with your arms and hang on tight. I'll get you down."

"I'm not even sure my arms can do that."

"Well, let's try," he said.

Immediately she slipped down to the branch he was on, linked her arms around his neck, letting her weight hang off his arms. "I can do this for a little bit," she warned. "It's pretty hard on my arms. Actually, hang on a minute ..." and then she bent both knees around his hips. "That I can do," she said.

"Okay, hold on." And he nimbly moved from branch to branch without jostling her very much at all.

When she finally saw the ground below them, someone plucked her off his back. With a shriek, she turned around to see Bonaparte, grinning, as he lifted her and placed her on the ground. Then he said, "Let me make this easier." Picking her up in his arms, like a two-year-old, he carried her, trampling through the underbrush.

Yet lightly, more lightly than she thought possible. "How can you move so quietly?" she murmured.

"I made a ton of noise getting in here. But now I'm trying to be quiet. For one, I'm used to moving silently," he said, "and, two, I'm not injured."

"True," she said, "but you are five times my size, so that's got to be a challenge."

"Five times the muscle so that I can pick up my body parts as I need to," he said seriously.

She gave up that argument.

He laughed and added, "Here is the car."

She turned to see that they were already at the side of the vehicle. Zack stepped ahead, opened the back door, and watched as she awkwardly made her way from Bonaparte's chest onto the back seat.

She shifted farther into the car. "I was so scared when

the other vehicle arrived. I was afraid the cops would come too."

"I'm just glad they didn't take the vehicle at that time," Bonaparte said. "Then we would have been sunk." He hopped into the driver's seat, pulled the keys from his pocket, and fired up the engine. With everyone inside and safe again, he quickly turned it around and headed down the road.

"What about my mother?" she asked.

Zack turned and explained to her what they'd found out.

"They are looking for my father's ledgers." She thought about that and nodded. "His office. He's got a big safe in there," she said, "but it's hidden. If they'd searched his office, they probably wouldn't have found it."

"Well, maybe that's why they want your mother then. She is still alive, but your father is not."

She took that like a blow and let her body sway with it. "It's not unexpected," she said, catching her breath. "He chose to be the man he is, knowing that the end result wouldn't be the nicest."

"And your mother wasn't doing all that good from what I understood," he said.

"Her health is declining, but she was trying to hide it from me," Zadie said shortly. "I've been hoping to get her out of there, so that we could get her treated."

"You know the outcome is likely to not be good, right?"

"It's a whole lot worse now, yes," she said sadly.

"So you know exactly where they are heading?"

"Yes," she said. "Back to my childhood home."

"And what do you want to do?"

She looked up at him, startled. "Well, there is only one

thing we can do," she said. "We have to go after them."

Bonaparte gave a bark of laughter. "I figured you would say that. But, just for the record, there are other options."

"Not for me," she said smoothly. "Loyalty, honor, family, friends. Those are all very important to me."

"Well, I won't argue with that," Zack said mildly. "But you have to understand the danger."

"I know," she said. "Same danger as always." She groaned, shifted on the back seat, and wished the damn painkillers would have kicked in better. "I don't suppose it's time that I can take another one, is it?"

He checked his watch. "Not for forty-five minutes."

She groaned and collapsed flat out against the seat then. "In that case, wake me up when we are there."

"Where?" Bonaparte said. "I need an address."

"And I've got it for you." She reeled it off as she laid here with her eyes closed. She heard Zack repeating it after her.

"I'm putting it into the GPS," he said. "Sleep. We'll get there."

"The question is," she said, "will we be in time?"

"I don't know," he said. "They already had a head start, and your mom is not in a good position here."

"So it's a kidnapping, outside of the fact that they also took and killed my father."

"True, but it depends on what's in those ledgers," Zack said. "Maybe they should be destroyed, so other people can't use them as tools against more people."

"And that's a possibility too. Actually it's a hell of a good idea," she murmured, her voice getting quieter. "If he's got it, and he's holding on to it, chances are it is ugly material and should be destroyed forever."

"Then maybe that's what we have to do," he said. "Now

sleep."

BONAPARTE GLANCED AT the rearview mirror and laughed. "Not too many women can drop off like that," he said.

Zack smiled, turning to check on her. "At least she is sleeping soundly this time," he said. "I was afraid the news about her mother would stop her from sleeping again."

"I think she's just at that point of exhaustion. I don't know if you noticed, but look at the color of her fingers."

Zack reached across and lifted her hands. They felt like sheer ice. "We should have grabbed a blanket for her," he said. "She doesn't even have shoes." The old socks were worse for wear from climbing the tree, not to mention the fact that they had little bits and pieces of foliage in them. "She needs more clothing, blankets, and she needs time to heal," he said.

"I'm not sure she will get that anytime soon," Bonaparte said. "We are an hour and forty minutes away from the address she gave us," he said, "so if you want, close your eyes and rest too."

"I'll take a power nap," he said. "What about you? Do you want me to drive?"

"Nope, I drive all the time," Bonaparte said. "That's the best way for me to operate in this world."

Zack would not argue with him. If Bonaparte said an hour and forty, and Zack's GPS said two hours and twenty, he would trust Bonaparte's assessment.

As it was, he had a power nap, texted Levi several times, checked the GPS, looking for avenues and routes for an attack at the new location. But it was a house, again a decent size, large, gated, with other similar wealthy estates around it.

"Nice to have money," he said, motioning at the screen on his phone. "Security, high walls, heavy gates. That figures."

"I guess. It sounds like her father was quite a piece of work."

"If he's got blackmail-worthy material on other people," Zack said, "I think it's important that we make sure of its disappearance forever."

"We'll at least check to see if something there needs to be made public first," he said.

"That's a judgment call that would be hard to make."

"I don't have a good feeling about the mother," murmured Bonaparte.

"Neither do I," Zack said, his tone quiet. Absolutely nothing inside him said the mother would be alive and well. "This is a fool's errand."

"It definitely is," he said, "but I don't see you telling Zadie that it won't happen."

Zack winced at that. "No," he said. "I can't say that I've gone that far."

"Not only have you not gone that far," he said, "but you are also looking out for her a little bit more than I would have expected."

He shrugged. "She's hurt. She's alone in this world, and she's traumatized. And now she's just found out her father is dead. Do you expect me to be mean?"

"Of course not. I don't expect you to be mean, but I see a *storm* developing."

Zack looked over at him and smiled. "You don't see anything developing," he said. "It's your French background to just see romance in the air for everyone."

"Of course I do," he said. "Especially for you."

"No," he said. "I've made some pretty irrational decisions in my young and stupid days. I don't see that any of my choices had been particularly an improvement on most."

At that, Bonaparte laughed. "We tend to pick a type," he said. "Until we realize how wrong that type is for us. Then we chose something that's good for us instead of a type."

"Well, I don't know what's good for me," Zack said with a chuckle.

"I think she's good for you," he said.

"Zadie?" Zack asked in surprise. He turned to look at his partner. "I don't know her very well, but she's got guts, and she's been very easy to deal with. She's got that weird, almost warrior thinking to her. But I mean, I really can't say there's anything between us."

"No, you probably can't," he said. "At least not yet. But give it time."

There was enough mysteriousness to his voice that made Zack look at his partner in surprise. "Now you sound like some weird little French seer."

"I have a good track record when it comes to things like these," he said.

"Well, don't tell Ice and Levi that, for God's sake," he said. "That'll add to their whole mystical matchmaking program they have going on."

"Works for them though," Bonaparte said.

"Maybe," Zack said, "but that doesn't mean I want to be another part of the program."

"Pretty sure it's already too late," he said, and he whistled the wedding march.

Zack glared at him. "On that note, I'll take another power nap."

"Sweet dreams," he said.

Groaning, Zack closed his eyes, and, despite his best efforts, he couldn't think of anything but the woman on the seat behind him. He went over the words and the actions shared between them. Noting a little zing of a spark every time they touched. How he felt extraprotective of her. But then she'd been through a lot. She deserved to have somebody look after her for a change, instead of her always looking after everybody else.

She'd been making plans to escape and to take her mother with her. He wondered about that because he really felt that, in her heart of hearts, that wouldn't happen. Mom would never leave Dad, and no way she could get Dad out of there. Now that Dad was gone, Zadie's worry was definitely focused on Mom, but, at the same time, Zadie had to know how dicey this would be.

Finally he opened his eyes and glared at Bonaparte. "It won't work."

"Sleep," Bonaparte replied. "Leave it to fate. If it's meant to be, it's meant to be."

He shook his head at that, closed his eyes, and let his mind drift. The last thought he had, thanks to Bonaparte, was all about Zadie.

Chapter 8

M AYBE THE DROP from the hell-bound speed signaled a change in circumstances, but Zadie woke with a start as the vehicle came to a rolling stop. Pushing onto her elbows, she stared out the windows. "This is the right neighborhood," she said, rubbing the sleep out of her eyes. "I can't believe I slept that long."

"You needed it," Zack said, turning around in the seat to look back at her. She smiled up at him. "You look much better," he said, his gaze assessing as he studied her down the length of her to her leg and back up again. "How does the leg feel?"

"It feels okay at the moment," she admitted. "At least until I stand up."

"Do you have any clothing at your parents' place?"

She looked at him in surprise; then her eyebrows rose. "You know what? I probably still do," she said. "I never even thought of that."

"I'm hoping we can at least get you some shoes," he said, motioning at the socks that were surely much the worse for wear.

She sat up awkwardly with her leg raised as it was and pulled some twigs out of the socks. "They did the job up 'til now," she said. "But you are right, it would be nice to have proper fitting shoes." She looked around, leaned forward, and pointed. "Go up two blocks and then take a left."

Bonaparte followed her directions easily.

She looked at him and asked, "How is it you have needed no sleep yet?"

"I had lots of sleep before the job," he said.

She shook her head at that. "We can't stockpile sleep," she said dismissively.

"You can do anything you need to," he said. "I'll sleep after this scenario."

"I still doubt he'll let me drive," Zack said, laughing.

Bonaparte shrugged. "I won't have any choice," he said, "but it's not my preference."

They pulled up where she told them to and parked. "Now, that next block," she said, "that second driveway leads into that residence, and that's my parents' house."

"Who owns it?"

"They do," she said. She struggled to turn around so she sat normally and then opened the passenger door. As she did so, Zack hopped out of the front seat, came around, and reached down with a hand to help her up. She stood up on her good leg, looked down, and said, "You're right. The socks have got to go." She smiled.

"Maybe, but how's the leg doing?"

She carefully put a little weight on it, hobbling forward. "Not as good as it could be. I was hoping it would feel much better."

"It might soon," he said. "What we need is to get you off of it."

"Now that I'm finally standing on it again," she joked.

He smiled, nodded, and turned as Bonaparte joined them. With the vehicle locked up, Zack looked at her and said, "We don't know for sure anybody is here."

"No," she said, "but I do know that staff lives here year-round."

"How many?"

"Husband and wife," she said. "Speaking of which, whatever happened to the housekeeper from the other estate?"

"We didn't have time to go to her house in the village," he said. "Levi's got somebody else coming in to talk to her, if we can't get back there in time."

"Meaning, my mother's kidnapping is more important than mine?"

"We have you," he said. "We understood from you that your mother's life was the priority."

She beamed a smile at him. "I'm really glad you made that decision," she said. "We can drive back to that village later. We can sort that out after this. But first, we have to go in here."

"And how do you want to do that?" he asked. "If your mother is being held inside, we can't just waltz in."

"True," she said. "But, if we go in through the neighbor's backyard, a small gate is between them. We can come up on the side where my room is and a big ladderlike trellis." As she spoke, they listened intently. "It leads up to my window. I've used it more than a time or two to get in and out."

"Must have been fun growing up here," Bonaparte said with a smile.

"My father was not an easy person to live with," she said.

His smile fell away, and he nodded. "Did he ever beat you?"

"No, he seemed to be perfectly content to beat my mother," she said sadly. "I think there were a couple instances when I was little where my mother intervened. It was almost like an unspoken agreement that he could beat her all he wanted, but he wasn't allowed to touch me that way."

"Well, that's one thing in favor of your mother," Bonaparte said. "But better if she would have left him than to have exposed either of you to that kind of abuse."

Zadie thought about that for a second. "I don't think she could leave him. She'd always been extremely vulnerable to his power of persuasion, and I know that she firmly believed he was the right person for her. So separating them would not have been easy."

"You didn't really think she would leave him, did you?"

She took a slow, deep breath. "I had hoped that she would," she said honestly. "But obviously I couldn't count on that." She led the way down the neighbor's side yard, which had a huge double gate with a circular driveway that went around to the back. The gates were unlocked. "These gates are always open," she said. "They don't have any kind of security system set up, and most of the time nobody lives here."

As they walked along the fence, Zack looked over at her. "That's quite a nice private area. The fence itself is what? Six, seven feet tall? And then you've got all these fine trees along with it."

She nodded. "It's one of the reasons why I worked so hard to leave in the evenings."

"Did you ever get caught?"

"Not by my father. My mother came in once, and I wasn't there. I had to tell her the next day where I was. But other than that, no."

"Your mother was okay with your behavior?"

"No, not at all." She smiled. "How many mothers are?

But, when I explained I had to get away when he started hitting on her or call the cops, she accepted my decision." She shook her head at the memory of the pain of watching her mother take the beatings, knowing that neither of them would thank her for calling the cops. "I tried calling the cops once," she murmured. "But the gatekeepers wouldn't let them in, saying that all was fine. Both my parents had to go down and talk to the cops."

"Ouch," Bonaparte said. "I imagine your father didn't appreciate that."

"I was punished severely for my *interferences*, as he would call it. ... I slowly realized nothing could break the weird relationship they had." She shook her head. "But now that he is dead, my mother should have a few peaceful years on her own."

"Maybe," Zack said. Just then his phone buzzed. A text from Levi. "He's got somebody who landed in Istanbul. He will talk to the housekeeper who imprisoned you. And her husband and brother-in-law."

"Good," she said. "Make sure their father doesn't get out of jail."

"He also sent a file on both your parents. Did you know your father had two heart attacks already?" Zack asked.

She looked at him in surprise. "No, I didn't know that." She thought about it for a moment, then shrugged. "They didn't tell me anything like that."

"Or how about the fact that your mother has cancer?"

"What?" She stopped cold and stared at him in shock.

"According to the medical report, she's refused treatment."

Immediately Zadie shook her head. "She wouldn't do that," she cried out.

"Are you sure?" Bonaparte said. "The treatment for cancer is difficult. Many people prefer not to go through all that pain to end up dying anyway," he murmured quietly.

She stared at him, then back at Zack. "She wouldn't do that," she repeated. And then she stopped and whispered, "Or would she?"

"According to the medical file, she already has," he said. "And she's only been given four months to live."

Her hand rose to her mouth instinctively. Even in the darkness, he could see the color washing away in her cheeks. He grabbed her free hand and held it close to his chest and said, "Easy. Just take it easy."

"It's an awful lot at once," she murmured.

"It is," he agreed. "You need to be strong right now."

"Sure," she said bitterly. "My parents were political prisoners. My father's been killed. Apparently he wasn't all that healthy to begin with. Now you're telling me that my mother is close to death herself? Basically, no matter what happens here, we only have at most four months to be together?"

"And that's if she survives this," Bonaparte said, motioning at the house up ahead.

She took another slow breath, closed her eyes, and then nodded. "Right, let's focus on giving my mom whatever few months we have." The two men exchanged glances. She frowned and said, "You don't think she is even alive anymore, do you?"

"Honestly, no," Zack said. "The kidnappers have no reason to keep her alive once they got what they wanted. And, depending on what they got from here, there is a good chance they might have left your mother behind."

"Behind?" she asked, as if needing to have it spelled out.

"Behind, as in dead," he said softly.

THEY DRIFTED STEALTHILY to the gate that she had pointed out. Since he'd spelled out what he felt they could find inside, she'd fallen silent. And honestly that was probably the best way to go. At the gate, she opened it and stepped through. But first, the two men stepped forward, checking the grounds for any danger to avoid.

She looked up at the ladder, which was basically a large metal trellis. "It's easy to climb," she murmured. "Or would be except for my leg."

"I'll go," Zack said. He immediately launched himself up the trellis and then higher. He climbed to the bedroom window that she pointed out, slipped inside, and stopped. The other two hid in the greenery below.

He checked the room and found it empty. It would be good if they could get Zadie up here but better not to go via the trellis route. It would be too hard on her leg, but she would likely try it if they didn't get a chance to slip her inside through the front door. He searched the room, gave an all-clear hand signal to Bonaparte, and then opened the door to the hallway. He listened, but he heard no sounds. Zadie had given them a nice verbal layout of the house from top to bottom, so he knew all the bedrooms were upstairs.

At the window at the staircase landing, Zack noted the small gatekeeper's cottage at the back of the property, where the housekeeper and landscape groundsman worked and lived. He checked the next bedroom, which was empty, and the one beside it as well. With any luck, the entire house would be empty, and Zadie could come in through the front door.

When he got to the master bedroom, the doors were closed. He frowned and listened hard, but still he heard no sounds. He quietly pushed the door open enough that he could peer inside. It did look like somebody was in the bed. But he wasn't too sure because so many pillows were there too. And he didn't dare turn on any lights yet, so the evening cast a shadowy pall about.

He frowned and slowly slipped back out again. He moved lightly down the stairs and to her father's home office. People had already been through the place pretty exuberantly. Files and drawers were everywhere. He raced through the entire downstairs and found nobody here. He moved to the window below her bedroom, part of the dining room area, and told them both through the glass to go to the front door.

There he had Zadie disarm the security and opened the front door and locked them in. He had her arm the security again. If anybody came and questioned why the men were here, the authorities would understand that the daughter had returned home. Zack motioned upstairs and said, "It looks like somebody is in the master bedroom."

She looked at him with a brave smile. "My mother?"

"I'm not sure," he said. "I came down and did a quick search around here, but I haven't seen anyone."

She nodded and headed to the stairs. "I need to go see."

"While you do that," he said, "we'll check the office for the ledgers. The place was searched in an ugly way. Drawers and files are tossed everywhere."

"Let me check on my mother first."

He glanced around and frowned because he wanted her to stay here, but she was already halfway up the stairs. With a look at Bonaparte, Zack pointed his partner toward the office, and Zack raced up the stairs to her side. "It was dark. I saw no movement, so I don't know if anybody is actually in the bed there or not," Zack said.

"Given the time of night, if they left her, then she could be in bed," Zadie chipped in.

At the master bedroom, he took a deep breath and asked, "Are you sure?"

She gave him a hard look. "The news won't be any easier tonight versus tomorrow. If my mother is in here, I want to know."

He opened the door, and they stepped inside. She called out, "Mom, is that you?"

She reached across to a light on a separate wall with a dimmer and turned it on, but she kept it low, just in case her mom was sleeping.

There was a form in the bed, but it didn't move. He lifted his nose and sighed sadly. She looked at him and frowned. He walked over to the form in the bed, turned on the light on the nearby nightstand, and stared down at the old woman, who lay under a blanket on top of the bed.

Zadie rushed to his side. "Is it Mom?" As she saw her, her face broke out in smiles. And then she got it. "Oh, my God."

Zack caught her up in his arms and held her close. "I'm so sorry," he said.

She looked at him in shock. "Maybe she is not dead," she cried out. "Maybe she is okay."

But he'd already confirmed no chest movement, no eyelid movement. Not only was she gone but she'd been gone for several hours. "She's gone," he said. "It looks like she lay down and died, or maybe she died on the way here with the men. They probably carried her up here, laid her on the bed, and covered her with a blanket, hoping it would give them some time to get away," he murmured.

She stared down at the form on the bed and sobbed.

"I'm so sorry," he murmured, just holding her close, letting her cry.

She whimpered against his chest, soaking him as her grief poured out. He knew that she'd already known this was a possibility, but the reality was always so much harder to accept.

When she was finally done, he reached over to the night table, took several of the tissues there from the box and handed them to her. She nodded and smiled. "Thank you," she said, looking around. "Can you leave me with her for a few minutes?"

"Of course." Zack stepped back. "Where is your father's safe?"

"It's in the office," she said. "It's kind of odd. It's built into the desk and the wall."

He looked at her in surprise.

She said, "Go find it. I just want to spend a few moments with my mother."

He nodded. "You know there was nothing you could have done, right?"

"Well, that'll be something that'll always haunt me," she replied sadly. "Because, whether there was or not, it's well past the point where I get to make that decision. It's too late for all of us." She sank to her knees in front of her mother, picked up her mother's hand, and held it against her cheek. "I'm so sorry, Mom."

"You might want to remember," he said, "that, if she loved him as you said she did, she will be happier now to know that she is not alone without him."

She looked over and gave him a watery smile and nodded. "I know all that. At least in my mind. But, at the moment, my heart aches."

"I'll leave you alone for a few moments," he said. "Please be careful."

She looked at him in surprise. "Do you think anybody is still here?"

"It's a huge house," he said, "and chances are somebody is possibly still around the property."

She nodded. "I doubt they are here though," she said. "Not when my mother is here." He hesitated, but she waved him off. "Go, see if you can find the safe," she said. "I'll be down in a few minutes."

"We'll leave as soon as you are ready." And, with that, he slowly nodded.

At the doorway, he stopped, looked back at her, but her head was bowed on the head of the bed, as she said goodbye to her mother. Something was so poignant and so sad about her situation that he could feel his own emotions catching in the back of his throat.

His own parents had been gone for a long time. A grief that he barely remembered as he'd been only nine at the time. There had been lots of grief back then, but now, as an adult, it seemed so distant. To see it so fresh and raw like this hurt and brought up his own feelings. He shook his head and called out softly, "I'll leave the door open."

She didn't seem to hear him, but then why would she? She was fully caught up in her loss.

He glanced around the room, making sure no hidden dangers remained. The closets were opened, as if they had originally left in a hurry. He checked the hall bathroom and the other rooms upstairs, then slowly made his way downstairs.

As he walked into the office, he saw Bonaparte standing in the middle of the mess, looking around. "Safe, what safe?" he said, shrugging.

"You can't find it?" Zack asked.

"No," he said. "What did you find?"

"Her mother," Zack said with a hard look. "She is dead."

Bonaparte's eyebrows rose.

Zack quickly explained what they had found. "There was no sign of trauma that I could see while she lay there," he said. "It's possible a bullet hole is hidden under the blankets, but it looks like she just laid down and died."

"It's possible," he said. "They could have poisoned her, but then again she could have been so overwhelmed with grief at the loss of her worthless husband that she may have just closed her eyes and passed on herself."

"Maybe," Zack said. "What we've got to do is find that damn safe."

"Yeah, show me where it is," Bonaparte said, "and I'll be happy to help you open it."

Chapter 9

IT WAS HARD to stand up and walk away, but she had no other option. Zadie didn't know how long ago her mother had passed, but her body was cooling. It was possible that she had died on the way to the house. That would have frustrated the men transporting her here, wanting the book of records. The fact that they had laid her on the bed and covered her up, showed a compassionate side that she found unexpected. Unless somebody else had done that. If her mother had laid down and covered herself up, that would make more sense, but, if the men had done it, what would be the reason? The only thing she could think of was that they needed to hide her presence longer.

Zadie was grateful that no signs of violence appeared on her.

If somebody peeked in here and thought she was sleeping, then that might give the kidnappers an extra hour head start. It would also explain why the kidnappers couldn't find the safe. She presumed they hadn't because of what Zack had said. That her mother had died on the way here.

She straightened, walked into the bathroom, washed her face and hands. Took another long look at her mother's body and whispered, "I'm sorry, Mama. I'm so sorry." Then she walked out of her mom's room.

She closed the door behind her and leaned against the

door and stared up at the ornate ceiling. Her father loved the gilded scrollwork that decorated the house, but Zadie loved simplicity. She stared down at the floor, noting the same carpet that had been here when she used to come visit years ago.

Her gaze landed on her socks again. She shook her head, limped her way over to her bedroom, and checked the closet to see if she had any hope of some clothing. At the very back were dresses and a couple sweaters. She could use both of them, but pants, leggings, jeans, anything tight that covered her legs would be difficult right now. Particularly being as injured as she was.

Now what were her chances of finding socks?

She went to the dresser, and, in the bottom drawer, she found several pair of jeans, leggings, underclothes, socks, and various T-shirts. With a smile, she took them all out, laid them on the bed and checked for anything else. She would need these eventually. The rest of the dresser was empty.

She took the clothes from the closet, brought them over, and laid them down as well. For her, this was a gold mine right now. She had no idea where the rest of her clothing was that she had traveled here with, but presumably it was long gone, disposed of by her kidnappers. Zadie traveled lightly, with just a backpack, and this stash would nicely replace most of that.

She also needed to shower. She frowned and looked around, walked to the night tables and found them both empty. And then went into the bathroom. She found toothpaste, toothbrushes, brand new, as if they had left them waiting for her to come home or waiting for another guest. Not too sure what to make of it, she walked back out to the hallway and leaned over the stairwell.

She heard the men in the office, but she didn't want to go all the way down there just to inform them that she was stepping into the shower and then climb the stairs again. Her leg hurt already as it was. They would surely hear the shower and understand. She went into the bathroom, grabbed several towels, locked her bedroom door, then the bathroom door, and stripped down. Careful of the bandage on her leg, she stepped into the hot shower. The relief of feeling the warm wet spray soak down her back and her sore head was incredible. She stood under the water, her hands bracing her against the tile, and she let the water pour.

She opened her eyes and shrieked.

There was Zack, glaring at her. She immediately tried to cover herself, but he shook his head. "I didn't come here to gawk at you," he snapped. "But what the hell were you thinking by locking the doors and not tell us what you were doing?"

She pointed at the door behind him. "Get out," she said. "You can yell at me later."

He turned, walked out, slamming the door behind him. That brought reality back home to her. Because, of course, he would assume something was wrong with the doors being locked. How her kidnappers could have left the water running for all he knew.

She turned, grabbed the shampoo bottle, and thoroughly scrubbed her hair. After it was drenched, she did it again and again and then again. With her body clean, just a little bit of blood flowing from her leg, she turned off the water and reached for the towels that she had stacked up.

As soon as she dried off, she wrapped one towel around her, bundled up her hair in another one, and opened the bathroom door. There he was, standing in the room, glaring at the window. "I'm sorry," she said. "I didn't think about it. I was looking to get clean clothes and a shower. I would have come down to mention it to you, but I realized going down the stairs and back up again would be too much for my leg, and you guys were talking and making so much noise, I knew you wouldn't hear me if I called down to you."

He held up his phone and said, "What about this? You know? Calling us?"

She looked at it, shrugged, and said, "I didn't think about it. I was still crying for my mother, just looking for a few moments of peace." She walked to the bed, sorted through the clothing, picked up a few pieces, and walked back to the bathroom. She shut the door in his face, then slowly and carefully dressed.

"How's the leg?" he called out.

"Almost better," she said, lying. "There is a little bleeding, but it's not bad."

"Let me change the gauze. You can put on a loose pair of pants afterward."

She froze because she had one leg in and one leg out, but he was right. Her bandage should be changed, and it should be a dry gauze. She quickly put on her bra, happy that it still fit, and pulled on a T-shirt. She wore underwear and still had the yoga pants halfway off. They were soft stretchy material; she rolled up the one pant leg as far as she could, got her sore leg through it. She opened the bathroom door, brushed her teeth, and pointed out her leg to him.

He nodded and said, "I'll see if I can find something for it."

With that, she finished brushing her teeth, grabbed a hairbrush, and ran it through her hair. Zadie scanned the bathroom to see if she could take any other items with her.

With a hairbrush, a toothbrush, and some toothpaste, it seriously felt like she'd won a lottery. All she needed now was a bag to put everything in.

She used to have some storage totes underneath her bed. She decided to take a look to see if they were still there.

As she laid her collections on the bed, Zack came back with a roll of gauze and some medical tape. "I found these downstairs," he said.

She was bent over and looking under the bed.

He walked around and squatted to join her. "What are you looking for?" he asked.

She didn't reply; she was busy pulling something from under the bed.

He looked underneath and pulled out what she couldn't reach because of her leg. A large plastic container. He flipped them all open.

She smiled to see more clothes. "Summer and winter," she said. "Now if I had a bag or two, I could restock all my clothing."

"What about in your mom's room?"

"Yes," she smiled. "She'd probably have something in there."

"First, your leg," he said. He patted the bed and said, "Sit down."

She scooched backward so her leg rested on her wet towel at the corner of the mattress. "It'd be nice to stay here for a couple nights," she admitted.

"And what about your mother's body?"

She winced at that. "I don't know what to do," she said softly.

"We can contact the police or whoever you need to in order to have the body removed and taken to a morgue or to a funeral home," he said. "It all depends on the laws here."

"I can call the family doctor," she said. "He could arrange for her removal."

"What about a funeral?"

"She wanted to be cremated and her ashes spread out in Mother Nature."

He looked at her in surprise.

She nodded. "As I said, she was a simple woman."

"Well, as soon as we get your leg fixed up," he said, "I suggest you make that call."

"What about the safe?"

"We found it. Right now, Bonaparte is breaking into it," Zack said. "But I didn't hear anything from you, so I came up to check on you."

"I didn't even think about locking the doors to take a shower," she said, shrugging. "After being on the run for so long, all I could think about was clean clothes and a chance to just destress for a moment."

"Understood," he said. "Next time, text me first."

"Will do," she said. "And thanks for bandaging the leg."

He nodded but didn't say anything. Finally he was done. He gathered the dirty bandages nearby, lifted her foot gently, and pulled out the wet, slightly bloodied towel underneath it. "We'll take these things with us because we don't want anybody to know we were here."

"I've probably got fingerprints everywhere," she murmured.

"But you used to live here, didn't you?"

She looked at him in surprise and nodded. "So then fingerprints would be the norm," he said. "In our case, we've been using gloves."

"Smart," she said, slowly dropping her foot and then

testing it. "It actually feels better after the shower."

"Well, cleaning up some of the dried blood would help not pull at the gash quite so much," he said. He looked at the totes in front of her and the stacks of clothing, and added, "Do you want me to go to your mom's room and look for a bigger bag?"

"Or check the closet here," she said. "I used to have some, but I didn't check the higher shelves." He walked over to the closet, opened the doors wide, pulled out another hanger with a jacket on it.

"There are some shoe boxes," Zack spoke, as he brought stuff down from the top shelf. And sure enough he found a couple larger tote bags. He brought them over and asked, "Do you think they are big enough? How long ago did you wear this stuff?"

"Years, but they should still fit," she said, as she looked at one of the totes on the floor. "If I filled one of those, can we take it with us?"

He nodded. "Do you want anything of your mother's?"

"That's something else I'll have to deal with too," she said softly.

"Do you know for sure who owns the house?" Zack asked.

"Last I heard, it was still ours," she said, "but I don't know what the will says."

"We found one, but we haven't opened it."

"No one has any news regarding my father's body, correct?" She looked up at him, worried.

"That's correct," he said. "It hasn't shown up on the wires as far as I know." He pulled out his phone. "But let me check with Levi to see if he's heard anything from the news media." He quickly sent off a text. "I've already updated him about your mother, so let's get you packed up as much as we can."

"Are you expecting the kidnappers to come back?"

"Wouldn't you?"

He helped her pack up everything into two tote bags. She smiled and said, "This is good. With the clothes I've got on, I can throw away everything that I came in."

He shook his head, brought out a plastic bag, and said, "Everything is coming with us. Even the old bandages, bloody towel, the clothes you had on, the socks, everything."

Zadie smiled. "I'd gratefully get rid of those." She walked back to the hanger that still had the coat, picked it up, and pulled it over. "This is also good for right now."

With everything packed up, and the room empty as far as she could see, Zadie walked to the top of the stairs, dropped her bags there, and proceeded to her mom's room. She went through the top dresser drawer, while Zack stood beside her and watched.

"She used to keep money here," she said by way of explanation. A jewelry box was off to the one side. She opened it, nodded, and said, "And these are real."

"Would she have left these behind?"

"Yes," she said. "She left a lot of that kind of stuff behind."

"Then we need another tote bag for you to gather your valuables," he said, checking the first closet, finding a larger tote, and dropping it near Zadie.

"She has a large jewelry case," she said, walking to the closet, opening the doors. "Let me fill what I can and take it with me."

"And then we must call in the doctor," Zack reminded her.

"I know," she said. "I wondered if we won't find the intruders first."

"You're probably better off to call the police and make this public," he said. "We'll tell them that this is how we found her when we got here."

"Good enough," she said, as he left her alone, closing the door behind him.

She walked over and brought out the jewelry box that her mom used to carry, hating how much of the jewelry was gifts from her father, who thought it was appropriate to drip his wife in diamonds, not keep everything in the safe, which just blew Zadie away. Although she wouldn't be surprised if she got them appraised and found out they were all fake anyway.

Packing up as much as she could of the more valuable stuff, she went through her mother's drawers. They were half empty, as if they had hurriedly packed. In the bottom drawer was a small book along with the family Bible. She opened up the plain little book, and it had no pages. All had been cut out and replaced with a thick wad of money. She took the little book and the Bible, put them inside the third bag with the rest of the stuff she would keep and went through her mother's closet, stocked with very high-end designer clothing. Some of it she might like to keep for herself if only for her memories. Also shoe boxes, purses, bags, so much stuff.

She didn't know how it would work in terms of the house, but, at one point, someday the place would have to be cleaned out. She was the only one left of the family to do it. With the box of valuables, she turned once again, walked over to her mom, leaned down, kissed her gently on the cheek, and then slowly walked out.

At the top of the stairs, she stopped and winced. Bonaparte stood at the bottom, talking to Zack, turned, looked at her, and grinned.

"Trying to come down the stairs?" Zack asked.

"I can hop," she said doubtfully.

He shook his head, walked up the ten steps, grabbed her three bags with one arm, then wrapped a hand around her ribs and scooped her up in his arms and quickly moved her down the stairs. There she landed on the main floor with a gentle *thud*.

"Thank you," she said.

"So this is all that's coming with us?" he asked.

"Yes," she said. "We should probably take it to the car, and this one is full of valuables." She pointed it out to him. "Make sure it's locked up. Otherwise I won't have anything going forward."

"Did you make that call yet?"

"No," she said sadly. "I was about to do it now."

"Come and join us in the office when you are done," Bonaparte said. He turned and walked away. She pulled out her phone and made the call that she'd been dreading for years.

ZACK LISTENED WITH half an ear, even as he stood and studied the contents of the office. He glanced at Bonaparte. "She just called the doctor. We should have company here soon."

"Absolutely," Bonaparte said. "Let's make this as legal as possible. I doubt anybody will get charged with her father's murder, but her mother's? I don't know."

"I highly suspect not," he said.

A few minutes later, he heard her on the phone again. He just raised an eyebrow to Bonaparte and shrugged. They had a whole mess of paperwork in front of them, and a lot of it wasn't in English. They needed her assistance.

When she walked in a few minutes later, her eyes were red-rimmed and a little teary.

He gave her a gentle smile. "I presume you've called the doctor?"

"Yes. The doctor had me call a service to come and collect her."

"Is the doctor not coming himself?"

"He is on the way, but he said it can take time for the others to come—and the police." She shrugged. "We'll have company soon." She looked around at the office and added, "They really made a mess, didn't they?"

"They did. We found these in the safe. Can you tell us what they are?" She walked over. One of the envelopes he knew was the will already because he'd looked the word up on his phone.

"This is all of it?" she asked, as she set it off to one side, and she went through the rest of the paperwork and several of the envelopes. She frowned. "This envelope, you haven't opened it, but he says it's valuable." She quickly slipped her finger underneath the flap and ripped it open. And out came paperwork, all sheets and ledgers.

"This is probably what the kidnappers were looking for," Zack said.

She nodded and winced. "We need to get rid of this."

He picked up some of the photos. "I presume blackmail?"

"Maybe. I don't know for sure."

"We can't get rid of it 'til we know what it is," Zack

said, picking up the envelope. "Let me take photographs of it. I can send it to Levi, and then we can destroy all these." He then picked up a box and handed it to her. "This was in the safe too."

She quickly opened the box and swore. "A lot of money is here," she gasped.

"There is," he said, "but no good leaving it behind."

She just nodded, and it disappeared from Bonaparte's hand into one of the bags she had packed. She looked around and said, "I don't know if I need to do anything with all this here."

"Open up that envelope with the will in it and see if it's how you expect it to be."

She winced, picked it up, opened it, and pulled it out, flipped through the top few pages, went to the last and nodded. "Two wills. One for my father. One for my mother. As expected, everything comes to me."

"Good," he said. "That makes it easy."

"Does it?" she said sadly. "This house has a lot of memories. I'm not sure any of it is good."

"You don't have to keep any of the memories either. I highly suggest you sell the house and create a new life for yourself, one completely unrelated to the life you lived here with them."

"That's a good idea," she said. She stared around at the mess in the office. "Do you think they found anything useful?"

"I don't know," he said. "I suggest we take the things from the safe. We'll sort it out later."

She nodded. "We will have people here soon, so maybe let's take these out to the car now."

Zack and Bonaparte quickly loaded up the contents of

the safe into a box from a closet.

She cried out, as if just remembering, "A vehicle should be in the garage."

"Good," Bonaparte said. "How long ago was it stored in there?"

She stared at him and nodded. "For a long time."

"Is it yours?"

"It's my mom's," she said. "I drove it for a long time."

"Maybe it's not even there anymore."

"I don't know," she said.

"That would be ideal, although that would be easy to track too," he said. "But that's all right. We can switch the plates and that would gain us a little bit of time."

She nodded and walked around the office. There were papers, files, envelopes, scratchpads, everything just tossed. The desk itself was broken; the books on the shelf tossed. "They really made a mess, didn't they?"

"They did, and sometimes people do that just as a show of frustration."

"I guess," she said. "Just a mess to clean up." She stopped, looked around at the trashed office.

He could see that finally all the dark shadows recently in her life had taken their toll. He gave a strangled exclamation, walked over, and wrapped her up in his arms.

She cuddled in close, and she whispered, "I'm not normally like this, but seeing my mother up there ..."

"Anybody would be shaken," he whispered against her auburn hair. "That's not an issue. Just take a moment. It'll be chaotic when the doctor gets here. And the police."

She nodded. "It's standard protocol." She looked down at her parents' wills still in her hand and said, "I feel like I need a digital copy of this."

"Do you think his office equipment works?"

She frowned and walked over to the office copier. She quickly fed both wills into the scanner and then added an email to the machine to send it to herself. As she stood here, she waited for her phone to buzz, and she brought it out. "That works," she said. "My dad always had to have a full office at home."

"Sounds like he ran a lot of businesses, whether they were legit or not," he said. "I'm sure he was busy."

"That's one word for him," she said with a broken laugh. She picked up the wills, photocopied them so she had a duplicate hard copy, in case she couldn't access her phone, and put them both back in the envelope. "I need to keep this close, and, as soon as we get a death certificate for my mom," she said, "I must make funeral arrangements."

"Of course," he said. "I guess the real question at this point is what you want to do from here."

Startled, she turned to look up at him. "Right," she said. "I didn't even think about that. Do you think I'm still in danger?"

He stared at her steadily, not sure how to formulate an answer. "I thought the guys who kidnapped you had a different reason than anything to do with your parents."

"Maybe," she said. "But I'm not exactly sure where any of that stands right now."

"Just take it easy," he said. "A lot is still going on in your world right now."

She took a slow, deep breath and then nodded. "I feel like I'm okay here. This is home, and I should just stay."

He stopped and stared at her. "Seriously?" He frowned.

She nodded and tried to explain. "I know you came to help me escape, and you did that," she said, "but both of my parents are dead, and that changes everything."

"And what makes you think that you are out of danger now?"

She shrugged. "No point in worrying about me," she said. "Since both my parents are gone, there is no leverage anymore."

"I wonder if that's true."

"I was looking at my bags, and everything I was trying to pack up, and it makes no sense. This is my home."

"But does it feel like home?"

She gave a bitter laugh. "No, of course not," she said. "But it's what I have at the moment."

"You will stay?"

"No," she said. "Definitely not. But I still have all these things that I have to deal with, you know, the estate."

"Agreed," he said, "but you can also get a lawyer to help."

"Potentially," she nodded, giving in. "But the bottom line is, I don't think I'm in any danger anymore."

"I'm not so sure."

Just then a knock came at the front door. She groaned. "Time to face the music." She limped forward and answered the door. He was right beside her. As she let the doctor in, he smiled and shook her hand.

"I'm so sorry."

She smiled and nodded.

Zack saw the tears once again forming in the corners of her eyes.

She wiped them away and said, "Mom is upstairs in the master bedroom."

"It will be okay," Zack murmured to her.

The doctor walked up the stairs, and she looked at Zack.

The doctor was only in there for about fifteen minutes, then he came back down the stairs. He again said, "I'm so sorry for your loss. Somebody from the service will come and collect her."

"Thank you," she whispered. "I called the police."

"It's a natural death," he said. "There is no need for any kind of theatrics about it." With that, he left.

She turned to look at Zack. "I don't know now. Was I supposed to call the police then?"

Just then, the police came up while the doctor walked down the street. She hurried out behind him and spoke with the cops out there. Zack watched, wondering if it was that simple. But everybody's country was different with rules that were different.

She slowly turned and walked back. He saw the police and the doctor getting back into their vehicles and leaving.

As she walked up the front steps, she looked at him and said, "I didn't want the police inside," she said abruptly.

He studied her for a long moment. "The break-in?"

"As long as the intruders didn't find anything," she said, "then I just want it all to go away. I'll clean up the house, put it on the market, and that will be the end of that."

"And you don't think the intruders will come after you, in case you have the paperwork they wanted your mother to find for them?"

"Why would they?" she asked, but her tone was muted, her eyes shadowed.

"Can you take that chance?"

"I have to," she said. "Otherwise I'll be looking over my shoulder for the rest of my life."

"You were kidnapped. So were your parents. Your father and mother died in captivity. The kidnappers were after blackmail material, which you are now in possession of. Do you really think they would not consider that? Especially once you've shown up here at the very house they already searched today?"

"But how would they know?"

"Because they are likely watching the house," he said gently.

She stopped and stared and then looked around nervously. "Do you think they are?"

Zack answered, "If it were me, I certainly would be. Remember we were supposed to leave right away."

She hesitated, then shook her head. "No, I will stay," she said firmly. "First off, my mother's body needs to leave and be cremated, and I have to deal with that."

"And what about the rest of the things in the house?"

"I thought I would haul all this out. The broken stuff can go outside," she said, "for the garbage, and leave it as an empty office. I'll empty my mother's bedroom, which would be a chore in itself," she said sadly. "Clean out the rest of the personal items and then contact a realtor."

"You want to do that while you are living here?"

She nodded. "Yes, I think that's probably the easiest."

"And with your leg?"

"It's getting better," she muttered. But she stared down at her hands.

"And you are avoiding looking at me, why?"

She raised her gaze to him and stared. "You came to save me," she said, "and I feel like I'm throwing that in your face."

"Well, we got you away from your initial kidnappers, but your parents were murdered by someone," he said, leaning against the doorjamb, staring at her. "I can't say that

I feel very good about leaving you here."

"Your job is done," she said with a laugh. "You can be on your way."

"Just like that?"

She gave a firm nod. "Yes, just like that."

Chapter 10

ZADIE DIDN'T KNOW why she suddenly couldn't leave the house, but she was sure it had something to do with her mom's death. Her mother's body was still here. Zadie just wasn't ready to say goodbye. She couldn't imagine that the kidnappers would think she had any of the materials that they were looking for, but Zack's responses made some sense, since they'd found the ledgers. Although what they meant she didn't know. Nothing was easy now. She really would prefer that he stayed with her, but she couldn't ask that of him. And she didn't want to depend on anybody. She'd been there and didn't like it much.

Zack stared at her for a moment, then said, "You can get a company in to clean out the house."

"I feel like I can't do that to my mother," she said. "So much of her personality is in there."

"And yet she is gone," he said.

She winced. "I know. If I can get you to carry the broken pieces of the desk outside, and anything else, then maybe just put all the rest of the office into boxes, I'll go see if I can rustle up some food."

She turned resolutely and walked to the big designer kitchen. She'd spent many evenings in here alone, cooking small meals. She wasn't sure how long it'd been since her parents had been here or if anything was even edible here. As she opened the fridge, she was shocked to find it fully stocked. That brought her around to the caretakers. She frowned and looked down the hallway to see that Zack had gone into the office.

Bonaparte walked in through the back door. He smiled when he saw her in the kitchen. "Thought there wasn't any food in there?" he noted. "We can pick up something on the way."

"I'm not going," she said abruptly.

He stopped and looked at her. "Say what?"

"I'm staying here," she said. "I have to look after my mom. I have to empty the house and put it on the market."

"And the people who came after you?" he asked and gave a headshake. "Not to mention the people who came after your mom and who were with her when she passed?"

"I don't think they will come back," she said, trying to sound reasonable.

"And why not?" He raised an eyebrow.

"Because they already came and looked at the place," she said. "They didn't find anything."

"Maybe they didn't, but that doesn't mean that they aren't watching you right now."

She frowned. "Zack said something similar."

"Of course he did," Bonaparte said in exasperation. "We are well past the time that we should even be here now."

"I'm not leaving until my mother is taken away safely," she said stubbornly.

He grinned at that.

She frowned. "I am not sure I'm leaving at all."

"You are leaving," he said. "But since we have to be here a little bit longer, see if there is food. And, yes, there are wheels in the garage. I've transferred everything over from my car, including the plates. I put its true plate inside the trunk."

She frowned at that. "But we don't have to go anywhere."

He shrugged and added, "I also moved the old car from your garage several blocks away."

She frowned even more at that. And then shrugged. "That's probably for the best."

"Absolutely it is." He walked over to the fridge, opened it, and rubbed his tummy. "I don't know how long they held them captive, or who is supplying this food, but it's definitely fully stocked."

"The caretakers," she said absentmindedly.

"Is that the house on the far back corner?"

She nodded.

"Did you contact them yet?"

"No, but I need to," she said, reaching up, rubbing her face. "I'm just not sure I can deal with the emotional issues of it."

"Well, particularly if you are selling the house, you have to give them notice. It's their livelihood and home too."

She stopped at that and could feel the tears and a sense of overwhelming gathering. "I can't keep the house," she cried out.

"I'm not saying that you have to," Bonaparte said. "But you will have to deal with the staff. It won't be an easy job."

She stared and then picked up her phone, walked over to a cupboard, pulled it by the handle, and inside were all the emergency phone numbers. She ran her finger down until she found the one she was looking for. Then she dialed the number.

"I'm calling Pedra right now," she said. "I can at least

find out when she last stocked the fridge because most of this looks fresh." As she turned around, Bonaparte pulled out eggs, bacon, ham, and what looked like sandwich fixings. "What are you making?"

"Big sandwiches," he said. "Some for the road, some for here. A lot of fresh food in there. We will need to take a bag to go too."

"I'm not going anywhere," she snapped. Her phone rang and rang and rang. She frowned and said, "They are not answering." She slammed the cupboard door closed and turned to lean back on the counter and stared at him.

"Are you expecting them to?"

"They are the older couple who live here full-time," she said, "so of course I am."

"Well, somebody shops and does the cleaning here."

"She does some of that. Especially the shopping. They have a cleaning lady who comes in too. I'll have to cancel that too."

"First," Zack said, as he walked into the kitchen, carrying the pieces of the broken desk, which he put outside the kitchen door, "you need to relax and get your head together. You are upset. You can't cancel the cleaning service because you will need it to keep the place clean while everybody is looking at the house to buy it."

"That makes sense," she said. "I don't even know who the cleaning service is."

"But your caretaker would know, right?"

"Yes." She picked the phone again and immediately hit Redial. They could all hear the buzz and the buzz as it rang so many times again.

"How old are they?"

"Late sixties," she said. "They were friends with my

mom for a long time, so she gave them the job here."

"Maybe I'll walk over and take a look," Zack said.

She nodded fretfully. "I would go myself, but I don't really want to put my leg through the walk."

"No," he said. He looked back and exchanged an odd look with Bonaparte.

Bonaparte gave him a quick nod as he pulled out bread from the fridge as well. He started cutting big slabs. "I don't know exactly what we've got coming," he said, "but I haven't eaten, and I need food."

"Make me whatever you're making," Zack said with a smile. "I'll be back in five."

He slipped out the door while she watched. "Do you think something's happened to them?" she asked Bonaparte.

Bonaparte looked at her and asked, "What do you think?"

Immediately her stomach dropped as she realized that, since the kidnappers had killed her mom, what were the chances that the caretakers were still alive?

ZACK DIDN'T KNOW where her sudden need to stay in the house had come from. But he presumed it was finding her mother and feeling that final connection to her last living family member. He could understand it to a certain extent, but it was not a good time for her to come apart.

As he walked out on the property, he noted it was a nice little cottage for an older couple and would probably have been a great gift in their aging years. But why hadn't they come to check on the obvious activities in the house, and why hadn't they answered the phone? In his heart of hearts, he had a pretty good idea why. But he hoped that the gunmen who had kidnapped her parents had more grace than to take out an old couple.

When he finally approached from the back, instincts had him going up to the window sideways, looking inside. No sign of anybody in the back, and, as he went around, creeping to peek through the side windows to check, he couldn't see any sign of life inside.

He walked up and around to the front, noting an old truck parked in the driveway. He rang the doorbell, but there was no answer. He waited, listening carefully for any footsteps, but he heard none. Putting his gloves back on, he reached for the doorknob, then pushed it open. The smell hit him first.

Swearing, he walked in carefully, trying not to touch anything until he found the old couple tied up in kitchen chairs, obviously beaten, and they both had bullets to the head.

He took a quick photo and sent it to Bonaparte and Levi. Then, pocketing his phone, he did a quick sweep of the house. His handgun was out and ready, just in case they had left anybody behind. Zack didn't expect so.

When he came back to the cottage's kitchen, he looked back at the older couple, his heart breaking for their brutal end. Because it hadn't been easy, and it hadn't been nice. A piece of paper was on the counter, and what it said sent chills down his back. It had Zadie's name on it, and read, *If you know, you better tell.*

He quickly took a photo, sending it to Bonaparte and Levi. When he stepped out on the front porch of the cottage, he stopped and slowly perused the neighborhood. He pulled out his phone and called Levi. "Did you get those messages?"

"Who are they?" Levi asked, his voice harsh.

"The caretakers on Zadie's parents' place," he said quietly. "Obviously the kidnappers brought Mom back here, whether she died on the way or not. The doctor said she died of natural causes, but that could be anything from a drug overdose to her cancer," he said. "She was dead when we got here, and I only just now realized the old couple were supposed to be here too, so I came to check on them. Zadie doesn't want to leave the house, and she figures she is out of danger, now that her parents are both deceased, so nobody should care."

"Yet you sent me a message saying you had the blackmail material."

"Yes, and I need to take photos of it, and then I want to destroy it," he said.

"It might be better off to just destroy it," Levi said.

"But it meant something to the people who kidnapped them," he said. "Maybe it's not about getting the materials so they can blackmail people too but getting the materials so nobody knows."

At that, Levi laughed and said, "Good point. So, as soon as you get back to the main house, make a digital copy of it all."

"I've actually tucked it into the vehicle, thinking we were all leaving," he said. "I'll go do that right now. Do you have any connections to the police here?"

"Why?"

"She sent them away already," Zack said. "They were here when the doctor was leaving, and she didn't want to let them in, didn't want to explain everything that happened to them. So, when the doctor said it was a common and natural death, it became a nonissue as far as the police were concerned."

"She didn't tell them about the break-in or about her kidnapping?"

"No," he said.

"Any reason to suspect that she is involved in this nightmare?"

"No," he said. "At least I hope not."

"Get us the blackmail material, and we can take a quick look," he said. "And, yeah, with the brutal deaths of the caretakers, you gotta get the cops involved."

"I'm on my way now." Zack headed over to the main part of the house and the big garage. "I don't know for sure what's going on with her headspace."

"Grief does funny things to people," Levi said. "She went there initially to rescue her mom from her house arrest. That was the plan behind her visiting her parents. Not only did it backfire but she got kidnapped, and her dad and mom, for whatever reason, are now dead," he said. "That can take a toll on a person."

Zack pondered that for a moment. It wasn't as if he didn't understand; he just wished he knew what he could do to help her, and he told Levi that.

"Send us the blackmail material, and then we'll all have a better idea," Levi said, hanging up.

Zack slipped into the garage, checked to make sure it was empty, and headed over to where Bonaparte had put all the material from the safe into the trunk. There, he brought out the 9x13 envelope, went to the workbench, and spread it out—all the papers, the documents, and the photographs—and took pictures of it all. A good forty-five minutes had passed by the time he finished.

He put everything back in the envelope and into the car again. He checked over the vehicle and realized that even the car had valuables hidden in it. Some money was underneath the false floor of the trunk, so it was hidden from view. Only someone who understood that there was space by the tires would have known to look; otherwise it was just bags of clothing and shoes and stuff. Nothing conspicuous except for that envelope. He left it there and headed back to the main house.

When he walked in, Bonaparte looked up at him, and Zack shook his head. He turned to look at Zadie, but she was busy making sandwiches. She added ham slices, then turned to look at him and smiled. "So were they home?"

"They were home," he said with a nod.

She stopped, turned to fully face him at the tone of his voice, and whispered, "And?"

He shook his head. "They were both tortured and shot." His voice was hard. "And a note was left on the kitchen counter for you." He brought out his phone and held it up.

She read it out loud, then turned to look back at him. "What the hell does that mean?"

Chapter 11

Z ADIE DIDN'T KNOW what to say. Everything overwhelmed her once again. "They were a really nice
couple," she said brokenly. "Sweet, wouldn't hurt a fly."

"That may be," he said. "They were also loyal, and they
may not even have known about the information that the
guys were looking for."

"No, of course they wouldn't have," she said. "They
would not have had a clue."

"That just makes it sadder," he said, "because, in fact,
they lost their lives over nothing."

"Now what?" she asked, staring, not even realizing that
tears poured down her cheeks, until he reached out with a
tissue and wiped her face. She snatched the tissue from his
hand and quickly wiped her eyes and then blew her nose.

"Call the police again," he said, "and, this time, tell them
everything."

She nodded immediately. "Yes, of course. I should have
done that in the first place. I just didn't know what to do."

"Well, it's past not knowing what to do anymore."

Just then a knock came on the door. She gasped and
turned. Bonaparte immediately slipped to the side of the
kitchen in front of her, while Zack walked to the front door
and opened it.

It was the paramedics.

She sighed, limped in to join them, and explained where her mother was. Leading the way, she guided them upstairs, Bonaparte and Zack following. The paramedics brought along a gurney. As the three of them stood and watched, the paramedics pulled back the blanket on the bed, lifted the frail old woman, placed her on the gurney, covered her up with a sheet, and strapped her down. They very carefully moved her down the stairs and outside.

Zadie followed them. Only when Zack put a hand around her shoulder, tucking her up close, did she still for a second.

"You need to let her go now," he said.

Zadie realized that she was hanging on to the gurney as the paramedics were moving it. Immediately she released her hold, and the paramedics loaded her mother's body into the ambulance.

It didn't take very long for the paperwork, and then they were gone. Just like that. She stared down the street and realized that her mother was no longer with her. She turned to look up at him, opening her mouth to speak.

But he placed a finger on her lips. "Don't worry about it," he said. "Whatever you are thinking right now, you are just messed up with grief. Just take it easy and relax. Let's go back inside, have a bite to eat, and a cup of tea."

She stepped forward and threw herself into his arms and burrowed close. She didn't cry. She didn't do anything, but she squeezed him as hard and as tightly as she could. He held her, gently stroking her hair; then he led her slowly back to the front steps.

"When do I call the police?" she asked.

Just then his phone buzzed. He pulled it from his pocket and said, "Levi just found somebody here in the police department to talk to. He said he's already contacted them. They know the whole story now."

She stared up at him, and her bottom lip trembled, and she nodded and brushed away more tears. "I need to get a hold of myself," she said.

"Well, maybe it's time to have a full-blown cry," he said.

She gave him a watery smile and walked into the kitchen. Bonaparte was busy plating the food and carrying the plates over to the table. The leftovers were on a huge platter, which he brought over next. She put on the teakettle, even though Zack nudged her toward a chair.

"Sit down. I'll finish the tea."

She sat down but stared aimlessly at the platter, full of cut sandwiches.

He got a plate, put one halved sandwich on it, placed it in front of her, then ordered her, "Eat."

She glared at him.

"Good, get mad," he said. "Get angry. Get pissed. I don't care. But don't mope. You need food. You need energy. We have an ordeal to get through. We have police coming. And we have to make a plan."

She picked up the sandwich and almost viciously bit into it. By the time she chewed through the first half of the sandwich, she placed another half sandwich on her plate. She went through the second one more slowly. By the time she finished with that, she sat back and said, "I think I'm okay now."

"I hope so," he said, "because we need you levelheaded and thinking clearly."

"The note was about the blackmail stuff, wasn't it?"

"I'm presuming so," he said, "but again, we can't be too sure."

"That's what they brought her here for, but she didn't tell them about the safe."

"I think she probably passed away before they could get her to talk," he said. "That's why they went after the caretakers."

"That makes sense," she said. "It's still not fair. They were the sweetest, gentlest, old couple. They wouldn't hurt anybody."

"And these guys don't care," he said firmly. "They don't care one bit, and they don't care about you, and they don't care about Bonaparte or me. They will kill us all."

She nodded. "And my name was on the note, wasn't it?"

He picked up his phone, brought up the image again, and placed it beside her. "Unless you know anybody else named Zadie."

She stared at it and shook her head. "Unbelievable."

"It is what it is," he said. "And, for that matter, we need to make plans now."

"Because you think they will come after me?"

"I would give it probably a 98-percent chance that they've been watching us," he said. "I suspect they are formulating a plan of attack right now."

She stared at him, her eyes huge. "You think they would really come here and attack me?"

"Unless you are prepared to put the blackmail material outside with a pretty bow and a note, saying, *This is what you want. Leave me alone*, I suspect yes. Also, they don't know if you can identify them or not, so your life is forfeit regardless."

Bonaparte picked up his fourth sandwich, bit into it, chewed then said, "The bottom line is, your life is worthless to them. And it's safer for them if you are not around to have anything to say in the matter."

"And they've already killed my parents, now the two caretakers, so what's another dead body or three?" she added.

"Exactly." She shook her head and said, "This is just unbelievable."

"Regardless, we need to deal with it and fast," Zack said with meaning.

ZACK'S PHONE RANG then. It was Levi. He picked it up, got up, and walked away from the table a little. "What's up?"

"Cops are coming," Levi said. "They picked up the housekeeper involved in Zadie's kidnapping. Apparently she was quite happy to tell them everything. She's worried about her family."

"Well, they had already kidnapped Zadie, so, yes, that would make sense," he said harshly.

"The one brother apparently is involved, and she wants him charged, but she wants to keep her husband and her husband's other brother safe and out of it."

"But she was also part of it."

"But she will talk in order to save her own skin," Levi said. "I'm pretty sure it'll all turn out to be a minor issue, considering the other deaths that have since occurred, and the cops wouldn't make a deal like that."

"Interesting," he said. "Well, I'll talk to Zadie and see if she is looking at pressing charges."

"I think her hands are full, but, yes, talk to her," Levi said.

As soon as they hung up, Zack walked over to explain what happened. She nodded and said, "I think she was just trying to save her husband."

"Brothers can be a strong influence," Bonaparte said, "and, if one led the other down this kidnapping pathway, then maybe it could be said that the one brother influenced the other two brothers, so just the one brother should be punished." He looked at her and continued, "How about you? Are you okay to let that all go? Your captivity?"

She shrugged. "I think I have bigger problems right now," she said. "As long as the kidnappers don't come after me again, then I'm okay with whatever the cops do to them," she said.

"Good enough."

She looked over to see Zack texting. "What are you doing?"

"Telling Levi how you feel about the cook, the female kidnapper."

"Good," she said. "Can you tell him to send some backup, so we can catch these assholes who are coming after me?"

"Not sure we need backup," he said. "Not exactly sure who is paying for our wages as it is."

At that, she gasped and stared. "That's right," she said. "Who hired you in the first place?"

He looked up and smiled. "Your mother."

And she burst into tears all over again.

Chapter 12

ONCE ZADIE STARTED crying again, it was just so damn hard to stop. She used the Kleenexes that Bonaparte gave her to dry her face. But the cup of tea Zack put in front of her was really what she needed. She took a couple sips of the hot tea, then several long, slow, deep breaths, and then she whispered, "I'm sorry. I just keep breaking down right now."

"It's all right," Bonaparte said. "Death of a loved one is a shock for anyone."

"I can hire you guys," she said. "I'm sure all the cash around here could cover your services, even if it's very expensive."

Bonaparte said with a big smile, "I work for free on the right cases."

"And it's hardly an issue right now," Zack said. "We already are here on the job."

"But, if my mother paid you already," she said, "I'm not sure that any money is left over to cover this additional element."

"*Huh.* How did she make payments for our services to Levi?" Bonaparte asked, lowering his hands to his lap and studying her. "How good was she at computers?"

"Very," she said. "And she handled all the bills anyway."

"So then she moved money around?"

"Yes, all the time. Whatever my father told her to do."
When the two men looked at her funny, she looked at them
in question. "What?"

"You do realize that your mom's probably the one who's
been hiding the money all over the place, right?"

She frowned. "Was there any money to hide?"

"According to our research, yeah, your parents were
worth millions," he said. "But a lot of it was in foreign
accounts."

"Right," she said. "If she followed his instructions all the
time, so maybe."

"So as long as they had access to a computer at *any*
house, including where they were under house arrest, she
could have taken care of things."

She nodded. "She did say something about getting
things in order. She could easily have done that with only
her phone," she said. "I know a lot of older people aren't
good with phones, but my mother was. She did a lot of
banking on it. She had different sim cards too."

"Where is her phone now?" Zack asked suddenly.

She looked at him in surprise. "I don't know. It wasn't
on her person. I know the ambulance guys checked her
pockets before they loaded her up, but they didn't find
anything."

"Might be something worth checking into," he said. "At
least then you could find the accounts."

"Maybe," she said. "That is more than I want to think
about right now."

"Understood," he said.

They heard sirens coming up on the far side. "That's the
cops now," she groaned. "I don't really want to face them."

"That's all for me," Bonaparte said, standing from his

empty plate. He still had another huge sandwich in his hand. "I'll eat and work at the same time." He looked over at Zack and said, "I don't know how long it'll take at the cottage, but the cops will have to come back here. You may want to put on some coffee for that part. By the time they leave, I'll really be running on empty. Before we make a dash anywhere, I'll need to crash for four hours."

"Done deal," Zack said. "And I can drive too, you know."

Bonaparte gave him a bright grin. "You could, but I want to get where we are going in a decent time." And, with that, he walked out the back door.

"I'm not looking forward to talking to the police," she admitted. "I don't know what to tell them."

"Do you trust them, or are they corrupt?"

She shot him a shadowed look. "I don't know," she said. "I know my father was corrupt, and that's a hard thing to admit."

"So maybe trust the police with the truth."

"I don't know the repercussions of that."

"Your parents are both dead," he said gently. "What repercussions are you afraid of?"

"I'm not sure," she admitted. "But I've spent a lifetime fighting between the two factions of legal and illegal."

"Where did your mother fall in this?"

Zadie was silent for a long moment as she tried to walk her way through it. "I'm slowly wondering if my childhood adoration for my mother blinded me, and maybe I didn't realize that she was more involved in my father's business than I had been willing to see." She sneaked a glance over at him to see the compassion on his face. She sighed, letting her shoulders sag. "It's only as we were talking about what she did on the phone that I realized how capable she was and how much money she moved on a dime at his instructions."

"And, therefore, potentially money that wasn't necessarily legally obtained, correct?"

"Quite possibly," she said with a sad smile. "Maybe I should check into that now," she said, looking toward the hallway that led upstairs. "Maybe I need to have a better look around her bedroom."

"What are you expecting?"

"Expecting nothing, hoping for some vital message from my mother," she said sadly.

"If she had her phone, how would she have sent a message?"

"Probably via a personal email," she said, and then she froze. "Actually we had several safe places that we used to drop stuff that we needed. When I ran out of money at one point in time, I didn't tell her that I was as short as I was, but she must have known, because she dropped ten thousand dollars into the account and then sent me this little note about what she'd done. It's like cyberspace storage, and she had put a note in there." She pulled out her phone and started picking her way through. "I wish I had my laptop," she said.

"Do you have a spare around here? Or what about your father? Is there a spare in his office?"

"There should be several spares in the house somewhere," she said, frowning as she glanced around. "It's just that it's been a long time since I've been here that I feel disoriented."

"No surprise there. You were a prisoner at one place, just as you tried to make an opportunity to escape, you get kidnapped. Then we rescued you and found out that your parents were dead, so anybody would be disoriented. Give yourself some time."

"Feels like there is no time though," she argued, as she hopped to her feet. "I need to see if there is a laptop around."

"Let me go with you," he said.

They headed into the office. She stopped, winced as she saw the mess, and said, "They didn't open the closet though."

"What closet?"

She stepped over papers on the ground, went to where the printer/scanner/copier machine was, and opened the cupboard that lay flush in the wall. Because everything was hardwood, including the wall, he hadn't noticed it previously. He stepped beside her to see stacks of copier paper and above it were three laptops.

"Okay, so not just one spare laptop," he said with a disbelieving gasp.

"I know a couple of these are probably older," she said, reaching for the top one. "My mom had a couple spares somewhere too. I'd have to go upstairs and look."

When Zack's phone lit up, he pulled it out and noted it was Bonaparte. "What's up?"

"The police want to question the both of you," he said. "So I'm coming in with two officers right now."

"Fine. We never did get that coffee on."

"I suggest you do," Bonaparte said in a joking manner. "The reception isn't friendly."

"Great." He swore, hung up his phone, and said, "Let's put these back, make it look like nobody's been in here. Bonaparte says the officers want to speak with us now, and the reception isn't friendly."

"Now that's the police," she said with a determined

voice. "It won't be pleasant, but we'll get through it." She straightened her shoulders, stiffened her spine, and led the way back to the kitchen. There she put on the coffee and began to clean up the remnants of the sandwiches that Bonaparte had made. She was still hungry though, now that she thought about it. She cut herself a fresh slice of bread and lathered it with peanut butter.

Zack came up beside her, saw what she was doing, and repeated it for himself, then he did two more.

She looked at the other two. "Who are they for?" she asked.

"Bonaparte," he said. "That man needs fuel."

"Well, if he eats the way he drives, there isn't enough food in this house for him."

"Remember. Answer the questions without volunteering anything. I'll try to give as much information as I can too," he said. "We are not trying to expand this investigation into anything bigger than it already is."

"The lesson my father always taught me was, answer with the least information, and don't offer anything," she said.

"Only tell what you have to tell," he interrupted with a smile and a nod.

"I just wish it was over with."

Just then came a heavy knock on the door, and it was pushed open. Bonaparte stepped in. She turned and smiled at him, as his gaze lit on the bread she had on the counter with peanut butter, and he rumbled, rubbing his tummy. "I was hoping there was more bread."

He strode forward, turned, and introduced the two officers who came in behind him. With stone-face countenances, uniformed and armed, both men stood and studied Zadie and Zack. Then one pulled out a notepad and fired off questions. She did her best, answering what she could. When she finally ran out of steam, they turned and started in on Zack. She poured coffee for the two of them and one for Bonaparte, deliberately not extending the invitation to the cops. She knew in a large part of this country, such friendship or socializing might have been the norm, but not here. And certainly not now.

She sat in place while the questions carried on over and around her. She looked at Bonaparte to see him studying her. She gave him a warm smile. "It's all catching up to me," she whispered.

"Do you need to go lie down?" he asked, concern clouding his voice. "When did you last have your pain pills?"

Her eyebrows shot up. "I've no idea," she said. She patted her pocket and then realized they were likely in the bathroom where she'd last taken them. "I probably left them upstairs," she said, yawning.

"Well, maybe you need to take your pills and then lie down for a nap," Zack said, turning to look at her. He turned back to the cops. "If there is nothing else, gentlemen, here is our contact information. You can contact us if you have more questions." Zack very determinedly moved the men back outside. When they were out and down the steps, standing and talking to themselves, Zack waited in place until the cops turned and headed toward the gatekeeper's cottage again. Then Zack turned and glared at her. "You haven't been taking your antibiotics either, have you?"

"I might have forgotten," she admitted. "It's not exactly been a peaceful couple days."

"No, it hasn't. Come on. Let's get you up to bed," he

said. He marched over to the stairs and waited until she caught up.

"What if I don't want to?" she asked. She started up the stairs and accidentally rolled her ankle over slightly and cried out.

Instantly Zack swept her up into his arms and raced up the stairs, carrying her.

"You know something? It's one thing for Bonaparte to do that," she said, feeling dizzy as the railing raced by. "But he is a whole lot bigger than you."

"He is bigger, not necessarily stronger," Zack said. He carried her to the bed and laid her down, then walked into the bathroom to check. "Yes, you left them here on the counter," he confirmed, opening the bottles, taking out the required amount of each, and brought her a glass of water. She struggled to pull back the top blanket so she could get underneath. He put the water and pills down on the night table, pulled the blanket back, and helped her stretch out. Then, while she was still propped up, he gave her the pills. She took them obediently like a child, then stretched out. He covered her up with the blanket. "Will that be warm enough?" he asked.

"It will be fine," she said. "I just need ten minutes."

"No, you need a couple hours, if not several nights," he said. "The leg won't heal if you are always stressed out."

"Well, it's been a pretty stressful day," she said.

He nodded. "Do you mind if I go give your mother's room a good hard search?"

"Doesn't matter if I mind or not," she said, "but thank you for asking. I know you would go do it anyway."

He gave a bark of laughter. "I do try to not step on people's personal toes, if I can avoid it."

She gave him a wave. "Go do what you need to do."

"Will do," he said. "Sleep well, and please don't disappear on us."

"Not planning on it," she murmured. And then her eyes closed.

HE TIPTOED OUT of her room, gratified when he could hear her slow, deep breathing. She'd been through so much in such a short period that it would take days, if not weeks, for everything to calm down. That she now had a missing father who was presumed dead, and a mother she needed to bury, not to mention settling the estate, there would be no end of headaches. Had the property even been owned by the parents, or had the government seized it as they froze all bank accounts due to his illegal political activities? If the property was in the mother's name, that could make things easier on Zadie as far as legal ownership. Especially if her father's body was never found.

Zack walked into her mother's room, turned on all the lights, opened the curtains, and systematically started at the top of the dresser, and worked his way down. He found all kinds of clothing, small personal effects, and some documents. He put everything in a pile on the bed and worked his way through. The first dresser was half empty, but the second one was full of winter clothes, heavy stuff. He checked behind the dressers for secret drawers, small compartments, basically anything that would hide any information that could help them.

When he heard heavy footsteps coming up the stairs, he looked out the room and called down softly, "Bonaparte? She's sleeping. I'm in here, checking her mother's room out further."

Bonaparte joined him. "This is ghoulish and opulent," he said to all the brass scrolls and heavy red painting and all the wallpapers.

"It's her parents' room," Zack supplied. "I found some stuff but not enough yet to give us any answers."

"What are the questions we are actually looking at?"

"I don't know," he said. "I just have a suspicion more is here."

"Good enough," he said. "I'll take the bathroom." He entered the bathroom, and, by the time Zack had gone through the second dresser and was working on the one night table, Bonaparte joined him. He went through the other night table. "All kinds of information here," he said, "but I don't really know what might be important."

At that, Zack checked behind the other night table and found something as his hands stroked across the wood. He took the lamp off and moved the clock and few other small sundry items, which he dumped into the drawer, and then he pulled it forward. "Well, things like this for a start."

Bonaparte looked over the bed and could see a taped envelope against the back of the night table. Zack quickly pulled it free of its tape, while Bonaparte checked the other one.

"Only yours has it," he said, "and that is the mother's side of the bed."

Zack pulled out the envelope and quickly opened it up, dumping the contents onto the bed. They were all pictures of Zadie's father with other women in very precarious positions. Zack whistled. "Wow! This is interesting. So she was keeping tabs on him."

Bonaparte looked at him, frowned, and replied, "Why

do you think?"

But Zack knew. "Remember? Zadie said that her mother was very busy with all the paperwork, but she was quietly abused for a long time. The woman I saw didn't have any bruises, so I'm not sure of the last time he beat her. But something like that"—he pointed to the photos—"might have stopped the beatings and had her take on a merrier role with the money. Maybe she was blackmailing him."

"That would be a twist," he said. They put all the photographs back into the envelope. "How involved do you think she is?"

"I don't think she was directly involved in these criminal activities, but I think she might have been systematically moving a lot of his money without his knowledge."

"For Zadie?"

"Yes, I think so," he said. "Maybe she was thinking she could get away. Maybe we were wrong, and she was planning to leave him. Or she hoped that, when he went down, she could survive."

"Well, the survival instinct is pretty strong," he said. "We still have to get a hold of the paperwork and the accounts."

"For that, we need her phone," Zack said. He put the night table back, placed it a little farther away, and then carefully removed all the blankets and sheets, lifted the mattresses, and checked underneath each one. Then they pulled the bed away and checked behind the headboard. As they moved to replace it, he lifted a pillow, and a phone fell out. "Eureka," he said and held up the phone so Bonaparte could see.

"You still have to get into it though," he said.

They finished their search and put the bedding back

somewhat right. He sat down on the edge of the bed and flipped through the phone. It was a pretty simple swipe combination, and, when he had it opened, he said, "I'm in. It's just a matter of what to do next."

"Check her email first."

When he opened up the email, there was a fair bit of business and personal stuff going on. He went to one of the search engines, opened it, and checked the history. Sure enough, banking information was all over the place. "Well, hopefully with this we can get into the accounts."

"Do you think that this property will be sold?"

"Depends if the Turkish government has a lawsuit against her father, in which case, they might seize the property," he said. "I don't know anything about that."

"I'll get Levi to look into it," Bonaparte said. "The best case would be if Zadie had enough to get started someplace else."

"If she could sell this place, it's probably worth quite a bit," he said. "But, between this phone and those photos, I'm getting a whole different idea about her mother. I'm kind of sorry she's passed on. I'd like to have talked to her."

"She sounds like she got a backbone somewhere along the line."

"Likely, yes," Zack said, as he tapped the photographs. "Nothing quite like a woman scorned. Especially when she has proof to show him." They gathered up the material they'd found into one pile, and he added the phone to it. "Now, the last closet," he said, looking at it. "I haven't done that closet," he said, pointing to the bolted one.

Bonaparte quickly went through it. They opened the big huge closet full of clothes and went through pockets, outfits, one after the other. "Very high-end stuff here," Bonaparte said. "Designer suits, designer shirts, nothing here is under a thousand dollars."

"You'll probably find nothing here under five thousand dollars, if not thirty thousand dollars," he said.

They brought down boxes from shelf after shelf and checked. There was one up at the far corner, which was a hatbox. He pointed up to it and asked Bonaparte to grab it. It was the last thing up there when he brought it down. He took the lid off and they both whistled because the inside was stuffed with wads of cash.

They looked at each other, and he shook his head. "This house is a gold mine!" he said. "Better put that over with the other pile."

And, with that done, he took another quick look through to make sure that they hadn't missed anything. By the time they had gone through the shoes and whatnot, Zadie's father's dresser was left. Knowing it could be another gold mine, they quickly but thoroughly went through it, checking out everything. At the end of the day, they found nothing there.

"I think this was her room for stashing stuff," Bonaparte said. "His room was in the office."

"Right, we have to check those laptops too. What do you think about staying here?"

"I don't know. She needs to rest," he admitted. "So do you."

Zack turned and stared at his partner. "The day is running out. Why don't you go grab four hours in the spare room? I'll check on the security system and make sure we don't have any uninvited visitors."

With the search ended, Bonaparte studied him for a long moment and then said, "It's probably a good idea. I need to crash." He turned and walked around the hallway to the far side where a spare room was. He opened the door, leaving it open, and dropped on the bed. He rolled over, pushed the pillow under his head, and closed his eyes.

Zack laughed. "You are one of the few people I know who can drop off to sleep like that." But Bonaparte was already past answering.

With him down and a stack on the bed already for Zadie to go through, Zack picked up the stack and carried it to her room, putting it on the floor just inside her room. Then he went downstairs, rechecked that all the doors and windows were securely locked. At one of the keypads for the security system, found at the front door, he read the instructions, and he found a note right beside it on how to shut it off.

That blew him away because, if you leave the code to shut off the security right by the keypad, that's like asking to get robbed.

In the distance through the rear kitchen window, he could still see activity around the cottage where the old couple had been murdered. The two cops they had pretty much kicked out of the main house were still working on the caretakers' cottage.

Zack went into the office and started searching. Now that he had a better idea of various things that were hidden around the place, he went through the piles of stuff, straightening them up, taking a look at various photos. He eventually put things back into the filing cabinet—in the wrong order of course because he had no idea the way they were otherwise.

But on one of the folders he caught Zadie's name. He pulled it out, checked out the inside to find it appeared to be a history of Zadie's life. He quickly photographed it to send to Zadie later, if she wanted to see it, then left it on top, and put the rest away. At least when somebody came in here checking the office, it would not look like it had been completely destroyed. He wondered why the cops didn't check out the house or at least this room when they were here earlier to take their statements. Zack had to wonder about their investigation skills at this point.

With everything cleaned up as much as he could, he went through the drawers in the cabinets against the wall and opened up more of the cupboards and found a strongbox in one. He unlatched it and found more money. Shaking his head, he put it back and kept on searching for more things.

And then came across another safe. He stared at it in shock because a big one had been in the desk, but this was a small wall safe. Usually if one safe was found, nobody bothered to check for a second one. Except people like him. Zack wasn't the best at safecracking, but he'd give it a go. It was a simple three-digit tumbler, and it took him a couple minutes to figure it out, but then he worked silently, hearing the tumbling on the inside. When he finally got it opened, he realized it held yet more documentation. He pulled it out, but everything was in Turkish. He didn't understand a word.

The file wasn't thick, but it looked important. He took photos of everything and sent it to Levi, then put it back and left the safe itself open. With the cupboard closed above, he slowly headed out and did another pass around the house, searching outside the windows to get a lay of the land.

The property had lots of trees and lots of places for people to hide. Going back into the kitchen, he made tea, and, as he watched out the back as several police vehicles pulled away from the cottage. Maybe they were done. If that was the case, it was possible their attackers would head in this direction soon. Although the cops had been a diversion over there, it might have been something he would have tried earlier, had he been the intruders. No real way to know.

As Zack checked his watch again, Bonaparte had had two hours of sleep, two and a half actually. Zadie's nap was a good three and a half, heading on four hours. But both of them were exhausted and could use twice as much.

He searched the kitchen cupboards for the tea stash, found something that made a passable cup, and, although he wasn't hungry, he went into the fridge, looking for more. He found a big slab of cheese, and he cut himself a thick wedge.

He wanted to go outside and check the grounds, but he didn't want to leave the two of them sleeping inside. Finally he settled on a chair where he could keep watch on the better part of three sides of the house all at once, full of windows.

When his phone buzzed, he pulled it out to see a message from Levi. **Call me.** He quickly dialed.

"Well, that's an interesting set of paperwork you handed me," Levi said. "The government of Turkey will be very appreciative of it. It would help them prosecute several corrupt people."

"It was in a small wall safe."

"Well, lock that safe back up and keep the images," he said. "I've already contacted somebody who will come tomorrow morning."

"Providing it's one of the good guys coming," Zack joked, explaining about the cops, about the cottage. "I think they are almost finished there though. There is no sign of any cop vehicles, but I can't guarantee somebody else wasn't left inside."

"That's to be expected," he said. "It takes time."

"The other two are asleep, so I'm on watch."

"Keep her safe because, given this political stuff you just sent me, if any of his rivals or the people he dealt with knew that this material existed, you can bet that house would go up in flames," Levi said.

"That's not something I want to think about," he said. "Did you look into any problems with the ownership of this house?"

"No problems. Her father transferred it to her mother's name about four years ago, so the government or the state shouldn't have an interest in the property," he said. "Zadie is the sole beneficiary of her mother's will."

"So it is her house?"

"Yes, and everything in it."

"Good enough," he said. "Quite a bit of stuff is here, and I'm sure there is more to find."

"Probably is, but you found a gold mine with that government corruption documentation, so you should take another run through the office and make sure nothing else is there."

"I haven't been through another whole filing cabinet yet," he said.

"If the scanner has an automatic feeder, just start sending it," he said.

"Some of the files are mixed up because the office had been destroyed. But I managed to get most of it back together again." He got up and walked with his tea into the office, turned on the light, and said, "I do have a whole drawer of files here," Zack warned him.

"Shuffle them into the feeder," Levi said, "and start sending them."

"Good enough." He ended the call, put down his phone, picked up the first file, and fed it through the scanner. He wasn't exactly sure where he would send it, so he coordinated the scanner to send to his email.

With that one done, which took about ten minutes, he went through the rest slowly and methodically. He repeated the process for each drawer. By the time he was on the third drawer, the last ten files, Bonaparte walked in, rubbing the sleep out of his eyes. Zack looked at him. "Feel better?"

"Yeah, I do. I needed that."

"You can grab four more if you need to," Zack said.

Bonaparte shook his head. He looked at what Zack was doing. "Are you scanning all that in?"

"Yes, I found another safe." He pointed to the cupboard that was still open. "Levi is contacting the Turkish government on some of these materials."

"Wow," he said. "I gather Levi decided they needed all this?"

"And we're afraid an attack will come from some of the other cohorts in crime. Also, no one has found her father's body yet."

"It may not show up," Bonaparte admitted. "A lot of places to get rid of something like that."

"But the house was transferred to Zadie's mother four years ago," Zack said, "so this place is hers free and clear, given her parents' wills."

"Yeah, sure. Mom had something on dad, and dad was toeing the line."

"Sounds like he needed to," he said. "And good for her because now it all belongs to Zadie."

"Good," Bonaparte said.

Zack scanned the last folder. "I've got this in an email which I'm forwarding to Levi," he said.

"Just to make sure we are not left high and dry if you

end up getting killed."

"Nice thought," Zack said, but he pulled up his phone, checked his email, and quickly forwarded everything to Levi. He smiled as he put away his phone. "Now my turn to crash. See you in four hours."

Chapter 13

SOMETHING STARTLED HER awake. Zadie bolted from bed, dashing to the door to hide behind it, before she could brush the sleep out of her eyes. Then the pain in her leg hit her from her sudden movements. She huddled in the corner of her bedroom, taking long, slow, deep breaths, trying to figure out what had sent her running. Her dreams had been filled with nightmares of her childhood, hearing her father yelling and screaming at her mother, her mother forever crying. To think Zadie was back in this house, her mother and father supposedly both dead, breaking her heart and stirring up things she'd thought were done with.

And yet it was all mixed up with guilt, anger, and frustration at the same time. No way to work her way through it all this fast. As she looked around, she realized long shadows were in the room.

Nighttime. Likely an hour or two or more before dawn. She let out a heavy sigh, straightened up slowly, and walked back to her bed. Detouring, she headed to the bathroom, used the facilities, and washed her hands.

As she walked out, she slipped over to the window and stared outside. The world looked peaceful. But this house held so many memories that were anything but. If it was hers, she was selling it. That was an instinctive decision that she knew she wouldn't move away from. Nothing for her was here. She wanted to keep things from her mother as mementos. But even now, she was wondering just how much she really understood and knew her mother. Had she been complicit in her father's dealings? Zadie didn't know. She hoped not, but she was learning a lot more about her mother's involvement.

She slipped back over to the bed and laid down. It was hard to go back to sleep, and her stomach grumbled. It was looking for food, which was ridiculous because she had had sandwiches earlier. But she'd gone days without very much to eat at all.

As her tummy continued to grumble, she sighed, wondering if she could make her way downstairs and get something without waking the men. Deciding to take a chance, still dressed because she never actually undressed, she went out of her room and slipped down the stairs. When she hit the kitchen, she stopped, surprised to see Zack sitting there with a cup of coffee.

He looked up and smiled. "I heard you coming down. Can't sleep?"

"Honestly, it's my stomach," she admitted. "Sounds like I need more food."

He raised his eyebrows at that but got to his feet. "It's five o'clock."

"Oh," she said in surprise. "Then I actually slept a long time. I thought it was only maybe three or four."

"No, it's five," he said. "We've already switched guard assignments again. There is a fresh pot of coffee."

She nodded, headed toward the coffee, and poured herself a cup. "But I need food." She walked back to the fridge and pulled out bread and cheese, making toast.

He stood up and asked, "How about some eggs to go

with that?"

"I was wondering about that myself."

He turned on a frying pan, and she passed him the eggs. They quickly whipped up a batch of fluffy bright scrambled eggs for the two of them. As they sat down with a hot meal, he said, "I should have thought that maybe your stomach would wake you up."

"We ate a lot of sandwiches earlier," she admitted, "but it wasn't enough to hold me all that time."

"When you're deprived for days," he said, "it takes time."

"Maybe now *time* is something I've got a lot of," she admitted.

"I left a pile of stuff for you to go through from your mother's room on your bedroom floor," he said.

She shook her head. "I didn't even see it."

"I took another look at your father's office and found a second safe. I sent some paperwork to Levi. It's fairly damning indictments against other politicians."

"Good," she said stoutly. "Send it to the government. Maybe they can clean up all this corruption."

"Already in progress," he smiled. "I've also been scanning in other materials from the office to send onward as well. Most of it in Turkish. Levi will have a translator read through all of it. A fair bit of stuff was here."

"Good."

He took a deep breath. "We found some stuff in your mother's room upstairs."

"What was it?" she asked with curiosity. "I'm half prepared to believe she was in cahoots with my father anyway."

"I don't know about that as much as I think your mother was blackmailing your father."

She slumped back in her chair and stared at him. After a
moment, she gave a broken laugh. "Seriously?"

"She had an envelope taped behind her night table with
photos of him with other women," he said. "And then we
have other documents. We also got into her phone, but we
haven't tracked all the information on it yet."

"And that means?"

"It means," he said with a half smile, "I think she was
using him to line her own bank accounts, presumably to
leave for you."

"And maybe to get away? We did talk about her leaving," she murmured. "But then I was persuaded that maybe
she would never leave him. But I guess maybe she was
planning to after all."

"I think she was. Bottom line is, it's very confusing, and
we don't have enough information to know yet."

"Maybe," she said. "But it is encouraging. I actually prefer the idea of her blackmailing him."

"Do you know when he stopped beating her? If he ever
stopped. Maybe some of that information is in the stuff
we've got upstairs for you."

"Maybe," she said. "I've also got to search to find out if
she left me any messages online. I was gonna do that on a
laptop earlier, but then the cops came." She pulled out her
phone. "I can do some of that right now."

"Only if you are ready to do it," he said. "It's pretty
stressful."

"That it is," she said with a broken laugh. "But I feel
much better now." She pushed her empty plate off to the
side and pulled her cup closer to her. "I still need to get the
laptop, don't I?"

"Yes," he said. "I'll go upstairs and get the stuff from

your mom. You go grab the laptops."

With that, they both dashed to get the stuff they wanted. They came back and spread everything out on the table. When she lifted the lid of the hatbox, she stared at it in shock.

"Did you know your mom stockpiled that kind of money?"

She shook her head. "No. I had no idea. I didn't know she had any money."

"It could be her blackmail money," he said. "You know the money that she was taking from him or that she'd forced him to give her so she wouldn't turn him in."

She nodded slowly. "And, if that's the case, I mean, as much as I'm confused about everything, I am more emboldened by her behavior then. It makes me feel better to think maybe she was fighting back and doing what she could to make a life for herself."

He smiled in understanding, then tapped the laptop. "Then let's see if we can understand more of this."

She quickly searched to get what she was trying to get to and then said, "I'm in the cloud storage that we use. All kinds of stuff is here that wasn't here before." She stopped, her voice breaking slightly. "A note is in here from her." She quickly double tapped the document on the screen to open it up. She could feel the tears immediately gathering at the back of her throat. "Well," she said, "this will be tough enough."

"Why is that?" he asked.

"Because …" And then she stopped, taking several deep breaths, and continued, "*Dear Zadie. I know this is too little, too late, but you are right. I should have left him a long time ago. The thing you don't understand is how I loved him. But even now, after all this time, I realize that love isn't enough. I can no longer respect or even like the man and what he is doing. When I realized how unfaithful he was, I turned my anger into something useful to get him to stop hurting me. Once he realized I had all the blackmail materials I needed to go public, he immediately stepped back and started treating me better. But I kept turning the screw and getting money to do various things. Every time I moved money, I moved half into my account and half into his. After thirty-five years of marriage, half of it is mine anyway. But, as we were getting deeper and deeper into trouble, and I knew that there could be no good end to this, I moved the bulk of his money into mine anyway. It's got your name on it, so there are no questions who the money ends up with at the end of the day. I would like to think that there is a better world for me at the end of this, but I suspect that I'm too heavily involved for it to even be possible at this point. Still, I want you to know that I did eventually grab some control and tried to make a life for myself. It may not be the life that I had thought I would have, and it may not be the life that I had hoped for, but it is what it is. Know that I love you very much. I trust you to make better choices than I did. The accounts that you need to access are down below. Enjoy."*

Zadie sobbed quietly. When a box of tissue was pushed into her hands, she smiled. "It's really hard to see how this all comes from my mother," she said. "It's not the same woman who I last saw when I lived in this house."

"Well," he said, "apparently she had learned this for herself."

"Yes," she said, smiling. "It's lovely to know that she finally came to a different place." She looked at the bank accounts. "I've never seen these bank accounts before." She pivoted the laptop and showed him.

"Do you have a bank account that you want all the money dumped into?" he asked. "We can move it to that one."

"We will have to," she said. "I don't want money all over the place like that."

"No," he said, "I wouldn't either."

She looked at it, shrugged, and said, "But it's not today's issue."

"Maybe," he said. "But depending on how many people know what your mother did, it's probably best to do something about it as soon as possible."

"Right. Well, all the information is there for log-ins." She opened up one of the bank accounts that her mother had used and gasped at the amount. "Over half a million dollars is here," she said in surprise. And, sure enough, her name was on it too. "Well, maybe I'll leave it here," she said, "as I have access." But she went to the next bank account number and opened it, and the next one and opened it, and each one had a balance greater than the other. When she finally got to one stationed in the US, she was shocked to find several million dollars sitting there. "I hadn't considered how rich they were," she murmured. "But apparently rich means different things to different people."

"And apparently you are wealthy," he said with a laugh.

"Yes," she said with a shocking surprise. "Apparently. And I'm thrilled." She closed it all.

And just as she did so, he said, "Stop. Make sure you forward all that information to multiple sources so you can access it whenever you need to."

"You mean, in case I can't get into the cloud storage? In case my phone has no bars?"

He nodded. "Exactly."

She smiled. "Okay, will do." And she quickly moved a bunch over into her own email and cloud storage. After getting all that locked down, and, just to be sure, she took a photograph of all the logins. "Now," she said, "what do I do with the money that is in this hatbox?"

"Did she say anything about it?"

She shook her head and pulled it toward her, picking up each of the rolls, looking at them in surprise. Underneath was a piece of paper.

"*Whenever there was a holiday I couldn't take, a birthday present I couldn't buy, a gift I couldn't get you, I squirreled away the money equal to the item. I figured at one point, one day, I would have a chance to take you on a holiday that you and I deserved to go on. If that day hasn't come, please do something for yourself instead.*"

She looked at the big box of money and shook her head. "So many times we were supposed to do something, it was planned, and then my father would stop it. Sometimes he would agree to let us do something, then changed his mind. How long has she been collecting this?" she murmured in wonder.

"It doesn't matter," he said, "but likely your lifetime." He put the lid back on the box and added, "We've got to get this, and the rest we found, into a bank and somewhere safe."

"Not to mention what I already have in the car," she said.

"It's all yours," he said. "It's a matter of making sure it's secure, until you decide what to do with it all."

"We can go to the bank today," she said. "Can you just walk into a bank with cash money like this?"

"Particularly after your mother has died," he said. "We

also have to get the wills so that we can make sure we can get all the paperwork transferred." He explained about the house being in her mother's name and how it passed down to her legally through her mom's will.

"Good," she said. "Then it's a matter of cleaning it out. I want to take some stuff from my mom's room. Other than that, I don't know what to do with it."

"Where will you end up at the end of the day?" he asked curiously.

"I have a place in California," she said. "It's just a small apartment, but I thought I would like something with a little more land, a little more bush, a little more country. And it looks like now I can buy that."

"Oh, I think so," he said with a bright smile. "I would definitely think so."

She looked over at him, smiled, and said, "Thank you."

"We did nothing," he said, "but you are welcome."

"Well, it feels like you've done a lot," she said. "And you did rescue me. That alone could have ended up very badly."

"The question is, where are you going from here?" he asked.

She pulled the laptop back to her, opened up a document, and said, "Well, I have a lot of things to deal with. My mother's funeral. I need to contact a Realtor. I need to get the house cleaned out, well, at least the personal stuff cleaned out. Transfer of title. And then what?"

"Bank accounts," he said. "And if you have a place in California, do you want any of the furniture here?"

She immediately shook her head. "No, I'd rather sell the house as-is."

"And honestly, you might be able to do that," he said.

They sat, discussing things, until she realized it was after seven already. "The banks don't open 'til nine, and I can't get to the lawyer until probably nine either." She checked her emails. She had sent a message previously. "I don't know what to do about my father."

"Until his body shows up, there isn't a whole lot you can do," he said.

"I can deal with the house first," she said.

"Your mother's note, do you know when it was sent?"

She looked up at him in surprise, went back to the cloud storage, and said, "Yesterday morning." She shook her head. "So she did this while she was still captive?"

"And she might have cleaned out your father's accounts too."

"The information should be on her phone."

He handed her the phone.

She quickly swiped it and said, "My mom has always been partial to swipe passcodes." She brought up her history and went to the banks and automatically logged in. "She did, indeed, transfer all my father's bank accounts to hers. Or at least the ones listed here are empty."

"So it depends if he has any others."

"That would be in his ledgers," she said with a sigh. "It's a sad end."

"But an easier one for you," he said.

"Yes, definitely. But, at the same time, after a lifetime, what does he have to show for it? His reputation was a disaster. Many hated him. Some revered him, only because of his corrupt ways of life," she said. "It's just sad."

"What's sad?" Bonaparte asked from the doorway and added, "Man, I'm starting to feel really good again." But then he looked at the empty plates beside them. "You guys ate without me?"

Such outrage was in his voice that she immediately hopped to her feet. "I'm sorry. I came down so hungry that I had to eat right away." He looked at her and his face gentled. "Because it's you, that's fine," he said, "but not again."

"Not again, fine," she said and laughed. She sat down again and said, "Besides you are such a good cook, I'm sure you can cook yourself something."

"I'll have what you had," he said. "Scrambled eggs and toast." He cut up four large pieces of bread, put them in the toaster, and got out eight eggs, while she stared in shock.

"You will eat all of those?"

"Oh, do you want some?" he asked, turning as he went to put away the eggs.

"No, I'm good for a little while," she said, shaking her head at the mess of eggs he had.

"Good, I can eat these myself."

By the time he sat down with his large mound of eggs and toast, she was almost comfortable with the amount of food he had prepared for himself, but it was amazing, extremely amazing. "Wow," she said. "I'm delighted to see that you are enjoying your food so much."

"Me too," he said with a smile. "Plan of action?"

"I have to hit the bank and go to the lawyer's office, and I need to contact the funeral home too."

"Where do you want to go first?" Zack asked.

"You don't have to go with me," she said.

"I'm going with you," he said firmly. He looked over at Bonaparte. "Haven't heard from Levi yet, since I sent all that paperwork. I imagine he is grabbing some rest himself right now, while he has translators poring over the documents. So we haven't gotten any orders from him for here on in."

"Then I'll hold down the fort," Bonaparte said. "Maybe

see if there is anything else around the house to poke and probe through. And you get her started on her list."

"Will do."

She looked back at the two of them. "You can go home, you know? You don't have to stay and babysit me."

"I'm fine here. We proved that last night there was no attack, but what if there is an attack tonight?" Bonaparte asked easily.

"But it's not likely, is it?" she asked.

"No way to know," Zack said. "Enough arguments. We stay together. It's for the best."

"Says you," she muttered. But she got up and grabbed the purse that she had found, already holding a copy of the wills, and put her mom's phone inside. Leaving the laptop where it was, she said, "Let's go deal with the things that we have to deal with then." He picked up the hat box. "What about this?"

"We need to take it," she said. But she opened it up, took out one roll of the money and put it in her purse, and the rest she told them that she would take to the bank.

"Perfect."

And what she thought would be two hours, took six hours. She already had an account, but the paperwork, the loose money also raised eyebrows. And she had to see the manager.

When all the explanations were done, everything was signed off, the money counted and deposited into her account, the death certificate for her mom showed up. It read *natural causes*, which she wouldn't argue with, but she was grateful. With that, the rest of the paperwork was taken care of too.

Next stop was the lawyer. That took another hour and a

half, and then she went on to the real estate office. With promises from them to come the next day, although she wanted them in that day, they headed back home again.

"I'm tired," she said.

"But we are not done yet," he said, holding up his phone. "We just got a message to go to the police station."

By the time they detoured to the station, answered more questions, signed statements, and finally got back home again, they found Bonaparte passed out on the couch, snoozing.

When they walked in, he opened one eye. "Did you bring food?" he asked.

She glared at him. "No, we brought home two very tired, frustrated people," she said. "Did you cook while we were gone?"

He gave a huge laugh, bolted to his feet, and said, "Nope, I didn't."

But as they walked into the kitchen, she found steaks out, marinating, a big salad in a large bowl, and veggies prepped to cook.

"I hope that is for us," she said. "I know it's early for dinner, but we didn't get lunch."

"We stopped and picked up coffee and a muffin at one of the street vendors," Zack stated. "But, no, that wasn't enough food."

"The real question is," Bonaparte said, "did you get everything you needed to get done?"

"I think so," she said with another yawn. "But, God, I'm tired." She stopped, looked at him, looked around the house, and added, "Any visitors?"

Bonaparte shook his head. "It's been quiet."

Zack's eyes popped up, and he added, "Too quiet?"

Bonaparte looked at him, his face leaned out slightly, and he nodded. "Yeah, you know some things aren't exactly what I would say peaceful."

She froze. "What does that mean?"

He looked at her. "It feels like we are being watched."

"So you think that they are waiting to set up an attack?"

"I think they are waiting for when we are most vulnerable, least aware, and then they will attack."

"And why?"

"Getting rid of witnesses and gaining the blackmail material they sought," Zack said. "I wouldn't be at all surprised if they come back to trash the office again. Maybe take whatever laptops and phones are available and potentially kill whoever is here."

"Great," she said. "When will this end?"

"Probably not until you've sold the property, settled the estate, and left the country," he said. "Even then, I don't know. Depends on how ugly some of this stuff was that your father had been mixed up in."

"In that case, Levi handing more over to the Turkish government, so they can round up some of the other problem people in the world, should help," Bonaparte said.

"But until then," Zack said to Zadie, "I don't think you're safe at all."

"Great," she muttered. "That is not what I need to think about."

"Maybe not, but it's what it is," Zack said. "Sit down. I'll put on coffee and start dinner. We can have an early meal, and you need to get to bed."

"Yeah," she said. "My leg is killing me."

Zack looked at her. "Are you taking your antiobiotics?"

"Yes." She shrugged. "I know. I said it was fine. But I

lied. I had to get through what I had to get through." She dropped the paperwork she collected throughout the day. "At least the lawyer is on it, and we'll get Mom's will sorted through. Of course, without my father's body, his will has to wait. So luckily Mom took care of all that when she transferred all his assets to me. All my dad's accounts had been cleaned out already, my mom having done that the day she passed on." She shook her head at that. "I still have trouble reconciling the mother I knew with the mother that I'm finding out about," she said. "I'm happy for her, but it's still a bit to take in."

"Maybe," he said, "but it's not necessarily a bad thing."

"No," she said with a brave smile. "It's not. It's heartwarming and it's brave, but, at the same time, it's exhausting."

"I can see that, but it's all good."

"It is all good."

DINNER WAS OVER, and they sat talking, going through paperwork, translating some of the documents, sending material back and forth to Levi and to somebody from the government who had contacted them. Basically a clean-up evening.

When she continued to yawn and couldn't stop, he said, "Come on. Pain pills, antibiotics, and into bed."

She groaned and replied, "I kept hoping it would get better."

"It will get better," he said, "but you are on your feet way too much. Remember? You were supposed to stay off your leg."

She just glared at him, made her way to the stairs, and

stubbornly hopped her way up. He shook his head as he came up behind her. "You could ask for help, you know?"

"Oh, I could," she said as she made her way to the top. There she stood, wavering on her feet. She gasped as he came over and wrapped an arm around her to hold her upright. "I didn't expect the stairs to knock me out like that."

He helped her into her room. "If you weren't so damn stubborn ..."

"I know. I know," she said, reaching out, kissing him gently on the cheek, and said, "Thank you."

"You don't have to thank me with a kiss," he said.

She looked up at him in surprise. "Well, the kiss is because I like you," she said. "I really like you. The words were the thank-you."

"Good," he said, giving her a boyish smile. "Because I like you too."

"So does that mean that we get a chance to actually visit if you come to the US?"

"Well, we are visiting now," he said. "So how about, after we are done here, and we get this all cleaned up, and I'm not on guard duty?" he said. "We can make arrangements to go out once we are in the USA."

"That works for me," she said with a smile. "Where are you living?"

"I've been visiting Texas for a short while," he said, explaining a little bit about how he ended up there.

"Interesting," she said. "What's it like?"

"Lots of wonderful open spaces," he said.

She frowned. "You know what? Maybe I'll have to visit Texas. Maybe it's better for me than California."

"I can tell you that it's definitely way less populated," he said.

"That's perfect," she said. "Now go away, and let me get some rest."

He nodded. "But this time, I get to give you a good-night kiss." He lowered his lips and gently kissed her, just a brief fleeting glance across her lips.

She shook her head, clamped her hands at either side of his cheeks, and pulled him forward. "There is no way," she said, "that *that* was a kiss."

"Well, it's a good-night kiss," he murmured.

She pulled his head down, and she kissed him thoroughly. When she finally pulled back, she murmured, "Now *that's* a good-night kiss."

"Hell no." He tried to find his voice. "That's a *hello, hello* kind of a kiss," he said, "as a heading into the night but definitely not a kiss to send me away with."

She gave him a cheeky smile. "We'll pick it up later."

"If you say so," he said. "But it'd be nice if you gave me a time frame as to when."

She laughed but didn't say anything. She closed the door in his face, leaving him standing here. "Don't lock this," he called out.

"I won't," she said.

He heard her close the bathroom door but was still smiling when he dashed down the stairs.

Bonaparte looked up, rolled his eyes. "What are you doing down here?"

"She sent me away," he said.

"That's just plain foolish," he said. "Get back up there."

"Why?"

"She doesn't really want to send you away," he said. "It has entirely to do with wanting to be persuaded to let you stay."

Zack laughed at that. "It's too fast," he said. "She needs time."

"Nope," he said. "She doesn't. And she is not looking for you to give it to her either."

"Says you," he scoffed. Still, he thought about it for the next little bit, knowing that she'd probably gone to sleep already.

They worked on paperwork, sending materials back and forth. "Looks like her father would be indicted and go to jail for many, many years," Bonaparte said. "They got four other names from our paperwork, and the police are picking up those four."

"Good," he said. "We still have the people who originally kidnapped Zadie and wouldn't let her leave. Who the hell was behind that?"

"Well, the Turkish government says they had nothing to do with it, so my bet is on one of those four names."

"How many have they picked up?"

"Everybody but this guy Mikao," he said.

"The missing one," Zack remarked.

"Well, let's check to see if he's got any property anywhere close to where the family was being held."

At that, they started pounding the keyboard again.

"Yep, his cousin owns that property," Zack said. "So now we know who kidnapped her and her parents, and we need to track him down, so we can make sure she is safe. And where this Mikao is now is the real question."

"Surely he has an idea what's going on now," Bonaparte said, "since I presume he hired the people to pick up the family. I'm sure he is getting hourly reports right now."

"But now we know who he is," Zack said, emailing Levi with their thought processes. And then he realized the email would be too slow. He picked up the phone and dialed. Levi answered, and he gave him the rundown.

"Good, the Turkish government is looking for him, so watch yourselves."

"Even if he gets picked up," Zack said, "he hired these guys. So he will have to pull them off, or they are still on the job."

"That's always a danger," he said. "Watch yourselves tonight. Once Mikao gets news of the other three being picked up, he will get desperate to make sure he is not included in that roundup."

"Well, he might get included," Zack said, "but you and I both know that he will do everything he can to weasel out of it."

"That means getting rid of the witnesses and the paper-work."

"Exactly." With that, he looked at Bonaparte and said, "I'll take the first watch."

"Good enough," Bonaparte said. "It's almost eleven. I'll go up now and see you about what? Three-fifteen then?"

"At three."

"Perfect," he said.

Bonaparte disappeared, and Zack sat down and read every translated note on the case. If nothing else, there would be information for the prosecutors when everybody was caught. Then he added to her work list everything she needed to do to clear herself of the funeral, the house, divesting herself of all her responsibilities here, so she could live a whole lot easier in the US.

Then he searched the real estate in Texas, just outside of Houston, looking to see just where and what she might be interested in. By the time he found a couple that interested

175

him, he sent them to her. Of course she was sound asleep, but it kept him busy, kept him occupied. Depending on where she wanted to go, she had all kinds of options. She didn't even have to come to Texas; there were other places to go too. The USA was huge, and, with her money, she could damn-near pick any place she wanted to live.

Just when it was time for Bonaparte to wake up, she sent Zack a message back, with a real estate listing that showed about ten acres, an old creek running through it. He smiled when he saw that and sent her a message. **You are supposed to be asleep.**

She responded. **I was until you sent me these.**

He sent a sad face. **Sorry.**

Come visit me?

Dangerous.

Maybe that's a good thing.

Not likely.

You on watch?

Yes.

How much longer?

Ten more minutes.

Then come sleep here, she typed.

Dangerous.

Scared?

Yes.

Ha.

He sent a happy, grinning emoji back.

Just then, he looked up to see Bonaparte stumbling into the kitchen. Bonaparte took one look at the silly grin on his face and rolled his eyes. "You need sleep," he said, "but I will understand if you don't get it."

At that, Zack bolted upstairs. As he walked into her room, she was sitting up with her phone in her hand. She smiled, looked at him, and said, "I wondered if you'd come."

"I'm here," he said, "but I do need sleep."

"Perfect," she said and patted the bed beside her.

He walked around the bed, came up onto the side, and crashed on the pillow.

"Are you expecting an attack tonight?"

"Probably," he said, "but I don't know when." He closed his eyes for a moment and said, "I really do need to sleep."

She patted his shoulder, grabbed the blanket that was atop her body, and tossed it over him. "Sleep." She snuggled down, turned her back to him, and backed up until she was against him. "We have other days."

"And other nights," he murmured.

"Perfect," she whispered.

He closed his eyes again and slept.

At least he thought he slept. It seemed instead that he was awake almost instantly, hearing something seriously off.

He rolled over, looked to see her staring up at him, wide-eyed. He slipped from bed, walked to the window, and peered down. He pulled out his phone and sent a message to Bonaparte. When he got a message back, he smiled and said, "Get ready."

"What do you want me to do?"

He led her into the center of the room, then said, "I want you to stay hidden up here. Preferably under the bed, in the closet, somewhere that nobody can see you when they first get in here. I see two men. Bonaparte said he's got two others. I'll be back in five."

And he disappeared.

Chapter 14

"FIVE MINUTES?" ZADIE whispered to herself. "Hell no." But the door was closed. She got up, slipped to the window, and peered out from behind the curtain. It'd be impossible to see her, and that she was counting on. But she also didn't want anybody coming up the latticework, which was how Zack had originally gotten into the house, in order to surprise anybody still in the house.

When she heard a *click* on the metal latticework, she knew that's exactly what was happening. She looked out the window, then looked around for a weapon. The only thing she had was the bedside lamp. She took it with her, but she needed to let the guys know. She quickly sent a message to Zack. She could hear him racing up the stairs, coming her way. He opened the door, and she held up her hand, pointing to the side.

He nodded, crept to the window where the latticework ladder was. Black gloved hands reached forward, trying to lift the window. When that didn't work, he used some tool, almost like a screwdriver, and popped off the lock.

She stared in shock. Zack looked at her, smiled, and nodded.

The window opened silently. Her intruder grabbed hold of the window ledge and leaped inside, almost with the smooth grace of a panther. Just as he was about to straighten,

Zack was on him. He knocked him to the ground, straddled his chest, and with several hard punches to the face, knocked him out.

She didn't know if anybody else was coming up behind him. She peered out the window, but it was empty. "I don't see anybody else coming up," she said quietly as she shut the window again. "Go help Bonaparte."

He shook his head. "I saw two guys. So where is the other one?" He grabbed the stockings she held out and tied up the intruder at the wrists and ankles before disappearing.

She used her phone flashlight to check his face, but she didn't know who he was. She took a photo, then checked for IDs, but he had nothing on him.

She sat back and realized just how persistent Bonaparte and Zack had been about this and how right they were. Here she'd been thinking that she was safe because her parents were dead, but, until these guys—whom her father had implicated—were also picked up, she wasn't safe. Maybe after this, maybe after tonight, she would be.

She waited for what seemed an interminable time, then crept to the landing.

When she heard another man's voice from downstairs, her heart froze.

"Better you sit back down," a man said, his voice hard. "Where is the bitch?"

She gasped and wondered what she could do at this point. If Zack and Bonaparte had been taken, what would she do now?

She heard footsteps coming up the stairs. She immediately bolted through her bedroom window, out on the latticework ladder. After years of experience, she slipped down to the garage and around the corner. She dashed onto the kitchen deck and slipped inside that way. At the corner of the kitchen, she stopped and froze, because two men held machine guns on Zack and Bonaparte.

One of the gunmen saw her and immediately raised his gun and said, "Come right now, otherwise I'll shoot him."

She immediately stepped forward. She caught Zack's gaze and whispered, "I'm sorry."

He shook his head.

The guy grabbed her and threw her to the floor between the two men. She called in out pain as her leg slammed against the hard floor. "Hey, that's not necessary."

"Shut the fuck up," he snapped, as he was about to give her another hard shove.

While the gunmen were more focused on Zadie, Bonaparte grabbed his captor's forearm and wrist and, in a move she'd never seen before, snapped it in half. The man screamed, the gun falling, but the gun was already in Bonaparte's hand. He fired a single shot and took out the second gunman's hand. Except Zack was already up and had him down on the floor. With these two gunmen down, and her sitting here shocked at the sudden turn of events, she looked at both men, but Bonaparte and Zack now held the machine guns. Bonaparte lifted the butt of his rifle and slammed it into both men's heads, knocking them out.

Zack called out, "Stay here. There are more." Bonaparte took off after Zack.

She froze. On a sudden insight, she grabbed Zap straps and tied up the gunmen. It wouldn't hold them for long, but it was something. As she waited, wishing she had some kind of weapon, she grabbed the nearby kitchen knife and held it behind her back as she curled up on the floor, faking it for the other gunmen. Only as she sank back down again, she felt something press against the side of her head. She turned to see a gunman had sprung from the hallway. She hadn't even known he was watching her.

He laughed at her. "A knife. Really? Don't bring a knife to a gunfight."

"I wasn't planning on it," she whispered. "I didn't want to get involved in any fight."

"Too bad. Your dad brought the fight to you," he said. "I want the material he had."

"It doesn't matter if I give it to you or not," she said. "Governments on both sides of the ocean have it already."

He stared at her in shock.

She nodded. "It's all been turned over."

"You fucking bitch," he snapped. "Get up. Get up!"

She managed to stand but kept the knife with her. The gunman was pissed off. He motioned at her to sit in a chair. She stumbled trying to walk by the two other gunmen, who were still on the ground. As he reached for her, she spun and stabbed him.

He stared at her in shock, but she shoved the knife to the hilt. He sank to his knees, and she whipped the gun from his hand and pointed it at him. She didn't have a clue whether it would fire if she pulled the trigger, but she wouldn't take a chance. She'd already done more than she thought she was capable of.

He stared at her and whispered, "You are just like your fucking father."

"No," she said, "I'm nothing like my father. I am, however, like my mother."

And he fell down, unconscious.

She heard running footsteps. She turned the gun as she watched, but Bonaparte came around the corner. He stopped with his hands up, and she realized how it looked. She immediately lowered the gun and said, "This guy caught me. I don't even know where he came from."

He looked at the third man and said, "And you stabbed him?"

"What else could I do?" she said crossly. "Have we got the last of them?"

He grinned and said, "Absolutely."

Zack came around the corner on the other side, carrying a fourth man. He took one look, smiled, and said, "Bonaparte, you want to go grab the one upstairs?"

He nodded and raced upstairs.

With Zack dumping the fourth gunman on the ground in the kitchen, he walked over, took the gun away from her, and asked, "Did you use a good kitchen knife?"

"Probably. It went right through him," she said in horror, not wanting to see the damage she'd done.

"If you just hit soft tissue, it goes right through," he said. "It's very effective as a weapon. He's probably not dead yet." He went over and checked him, nodded, and said, "He is still breathing. I'm calling for an ambulance and the police," he said, "and I'm contacting Levi, so we can get the right government people in on this one."

By the time Bonaparte came back down with the fifth gunman still unconscious, an ambulance was on its way. And so were the cops. Levi had phoned his local contacts, and more people would be coming too. Zack looked over at Bonaparte and said, "Well, it's not exactly morning," he said, "but I'd say the day got started."

Bonaparte walked to the coffeemaker and quickly put on a pot. Before it even finished dripping, they heard sirens and ambulances. And chaos reigned.

ZACK HELD ZADIE close, noting the pallor and the shakes running up and down her body. Probably from shock. They were sitting together on the kitchen bench, with her sitting between his legs, held between his arms. She leaned back against him and whispered, "Is this almost done?"

"I hope so," he said. "I don't know about you, but it's getting pretty old."

She snorted. "You think?" She picked up her phone and sent him yet another real estate listing.

"This one is in New Mexico. And I sent you one from Texas."

"I guess I have to find a location, don't I?"

"Not today, you don't," he said easily. "Right now, we will deal with the mess we've got here."

All the gunmen had been picked up and removed, nobody dead, which was something that she was grateful for.

Zack, on the other hand, didn't give a shit. These five were hired dogs. So, as far as he was concerned, whatever happened, happened. Besides, they likely had a hand in killing the old couple, not to mention Zadie's parents. "Did we find out if the Mikao guy was picked up?"

"Apparently, yes," Bonaparte said as his phone rang. And he checked the message. He held it out. It was from Levi, saying, "Four for four."

"Perfect," she said. "So, once the cops leave, I can go back to bed?"

"Yeah," Zack said. "Me too."

She twisted, kissed him on the cheek, and said, "Let me rephrase that. Can *we* go back to bed?"

He chuckled and tucked her up close. "Yes."

It took another hour, and finally it was done. With everyone gone, the house locked up, Bonaparte shook his head and said, "I'm going back to bed. I, at least, will sleep."

"So are we," she said.

Under his breath, Zack whispered, "Eventually."

She chuckled and said, "You have to be nice to my leg."

"No, I have to be careful with your leg," he said, "but other than that ..."

Once in her bedroom, she stopped and yawned. "God," she said, "I'm exhausted."

Immediately he froze, looked at her, and stripped down. "Get into bed," he said. "We have lots of time ahead of us. There is no rush right now."

"No," she said, slowly undressing, "there isn't. There is a sense of keyed-up worry, like just a pit in my stomach that says it isn't over."

"Let's just say, it's aftershock and worry," he said. "It's over. We've got them all."

"Are you sure?" she asked. She stood nude in front of him, except for the gauze bandage on her injured leg.

He smiled and said, "You're absolutely gorgeous dressed like that. Did you know that?"

"Wearing only this?" She looked down, gave her leg a gentle shimmy, and said, "You like that, huh?" She walked over, looped her hands around his neck, pressing her body against him tightly, from their chests to their hips, heated skin to heated skin. "I think you are perfectly dressed."

"Our birthday suits are all we need." He nodded in agreement and picked her up gently, laid her down on the bed, and said, "Sleep?"

"Later," she whispered, "definitely later. One of the lessons this whole mess taught me is that life happens when you were doing something else, and it's important to stop, relax, and enjoy what counts because sometimes *tomorrow* just doesn't happen."

He reached down, kissed her gently, and said, "As long as you're sure."

"I'm sure," she whispered, pulling him down on top of her.

Skin to skin, heart to heart, mind to mind, the two of them kissed with a passion that he hadn't expected, hadn't been looking for, and even now was stunned at the sense of homecoming he felt inside. He kissed her hard, feeling his own response rising up with a need he hadn't expected. It was more than sex, more than a coming together after a horrible event. It was so ... very much more.

She moaned underneath him.

"I don't want to hurt your leg."

He held her beside him and then tightened in closer until they lay on their sides. Each of them gently exploring, both too tired, both too stressed, both too wound up for too much activity, and yet needing to take this step. Needing to have this commitment, needing to cross this bridge, and wanting, desperately wanting, the fulfillment that came with the release of knowing both of them were in it together.

It didn't take much before he was groaning and pushing her gently onto her back, her bad leg hanging off the side of the bed as he whispered, "How about this?"

"That would work too," she said, "but you're worrying too much."

"No," he said, "I'll never forgive myself if I hurt you." But when he finally slipped deep inside her, it was all he could do to retain any sense of control. This woman twisting beneath him was just so damn sexy and wanton in her own needs that all he wanted to do was pleasure her over and over again.

When she finally lurched up against him and pulled him down hard and whispered, "Move, damn it, or I'll make you move."

He drove deep and let his own passion take over. He drove deeper, harder, and faster. When he'd finally burst, his own pleasure whipping through him, he slid a finger down between them, gently caressing her until she cried out beneath him. He collapsed to her side, pulled her deep into his arms, and whispered, "Now sleep. We have time for more tomorrow."

"You mean in a little while," she whispered. "Because today is not even over yet. And I intend to revisit this again and again."

"When we are rested," he promised.

"As long as you don't use my leg for an excuse."

"That's not happening," he said. "But rest now."

She looped her arms around his neck, snuggled in close, and whispered, "Yes, boss."

He chuckled. "That'll be the only time you follow orders, isn't it?"

"Absolutely," she said with a chuckle, and she closed her eyes and slept.

He tucked her up close, and his phone buzzed at that. He reached across to the night table, lifted his phone to see Levi's text.

Spend a few days and enjoy life. It's too short, so take the time when you have it.

Zack texted with one finger a simple message back, typing, **I am.**

He sent off the message, crawled beside Zadie, and slept.

His last thought was that Levi's matchmaking magic had worked again.

Epilogue

B ONAPARTE GASPARDE WAS happy for Zack and Zadie. It's not what Bonaparte had expected when they'd started this mission, but, once he'd seen the sparks flying between the two of them, Bonaparte knew that there would be no other way that this ended. Zack looked like he had a whole new lease on life. Bonaparte was happy for his friend.

Bonaparte had returned to the States with them and had spent a few weeks lost until Levi suggested Bonaparte stay and do a couple jobs, 'til he figured out what he wanted to do.

Being here was hard in a way. His self-introspection into his prior relationship was brutal. Yet he'd seen so many beautiful couples at Levi's place that Bonaparte wondered if he was half inclined to be here, just so some of that pixie dust might fall his way.

Just then Levi walked into the kitchen. "Is everything well with you?"

"I'm good," Bonaparte said.

"Well, how do you feel about heading outside of Denver to help out a friend?"

"What's there?"

"Another case gone wrong." Levi sighed. "This is actually a favor for the new sheriff of a small town."

"What kind of a problem? Need a bodyguard or what?"

"No, nothing like that," he said. "The sheriff needs someone to deputize for the short-term, having told a bunch of guys that new staff members were coming in, so they're expecting somebody, yet nobody is on the way."

"So, I'm just like a relief deputy for what? A week or two?" He shrugged. "Whatever. I've never been in that role before. How hard can it be?"

"Yeah, but you're walking into a trap," he said. "It's one of the reasons for saying backup was coming, but it's also one of the reasons not to actually get backup. It's a dangerous situation, and anybody the sheriff brings in could get their head chopped off."

"Great," Bonaparte said, straightening up with a big grin. "Sounds like my kind of job. Who's the sheriff?"

"Her name is Angela Zimmerman," Levi said. "She's hell on wheels, and she's an old friend. Do what you can to keep her alive."

"A female sheriff, sounds like fun."

"Angela is good people. She comes down on the side of right every time. And she's in trouble."

Bonaparte pursed his lips. He had no reason not to go. In fact, it would be better than sitting here and reviewing his failed past relationships.

"Don't let one poisonous nutcase spoil you for all the beautiful flowers out there."

Bonaparte laughed at that. "I doubt Ice would appreciate being called a flower. And I don't view my ex like that."

"So true," Levi said with a grin. "And good on the ex. Now go give Angela a hand." He stood. "At the bare minimum, this job should keep you busy, and you love helping the underdog. I can guarantee you that Angela needs you."

"Well, when you put it that way, how can I refuse?"

This concludes Book 23 of Heroes for Hire: Zack's Zest.

Read about Bonaparte's Belle: Heroes for Hire, Book 24

Heroes for Hire: Bonaparte's Belle (Book #24)

Sheriff Angela Zimmerman is not what Bonaparte expects when he arrives in her district. But he was here to help her out at Levi's request. A little matchmaking by Levi was going on too but didn't change the fact that she was in trouble.

When Levi said he was sending a man over, she didn't realize he meant this gentle mountain of a man. Still Bonaparte was confident and capable, and that's what mattered. Something rotten was happening in her town, and getting to the bottom of it alone was nearly impossible. Especially when all her deputies had been coerced to quit.

Sensing something much bigger was going on is one thing, but proving it is another. So the two set out to get the proof they need—no matter the danger. No one expected what they found …

Find Book 24 here!

To find out more visit Dale Mayer's website.

http://smarturl.it/DMSBona

Other Military Series by Dale Mayer

SEALs of Honor

Heroes for Hire

SEALs of Steel

The K9 Files

The Mavericks

Bullards Battle

Hathaway House

Terkel's Team

Ryland's Reach: Bullard's Battle (Book #1)

Welcome to a new stand-alone but interconnected series from Dale Mayer. This is Bullard's story—and that of his team's. All raw, rough, incredibly capable men who have one goal: to find out who was behind the attack on their leader, before the attacker, or attackers, return to finish the job.

Stay tuned for more nonstop action as the men narrow down their suspects … and find a way to let love back into their own empty lives.

His rescue from the ocean after a horrible plane explosion was his top priority, in any way, shape, or form. A small sailboat and a nurse to do the job was more than Ryland hoped for.

When Tabi somehow drags him and his buddy Garret onboard and surprisingly gets them to a naval ship close by, Ryland figures he'd used up all his luck and his friend's too. Sure enough, those who attacked the plane they were in weren't content to let him slowly die in the ocean. No. Surviving had made him a target all over again.

Tabi isn't expecting her sailing holiday to include the rescue of two badly injured men and then to end with the loss of her beloved sailboat. Her instincts save them, but now she finds it tough to let them go—even as more of Bullard's team members come to them—until it becomes apparent that not only are Bullard and his men still targets ... but she is too.

B ULLARD CHECKED THAT the helicopter was loaded with their bags and that his men were ready to leave.

He walked back one more time, his gaze on Ice. She'd never looked happier, never looked more perfect. His heart ached, but he knew she remained a caring friend and always would be. He opened his arms; she ran into them, and he held her close, whispering, "The offer still stands."

She leaned back and smiled up at him. "Maybe if and when Levi's been gone for a long enough time for me to forget," she said in all seriousness.

"That's not happening. You two, now three, will live long and happy lives together," he said, smiling down at the woman knew to be the most beautiful, inside and out. She would never be his, but he always kept a little corner of his heart open and available, in case she wanted to surprise him and to slide inside.

And then he realized she'd already been a part of his heart all this time. That was a good ten to fifteen years by now. But she kept herself in the friend category, and he understood because she and Levi, partners and now parents, were perfect together.

Bullard reached out and shook Levi's hand. "It was a hell of a blast," he said. "When you guys do a big splash, you really do a *big* splash."

Ice laughed. "A few days at home sounds perfect for me now."

"It looks great," he said, his hands on his hips as he surveyed the people in the massive pool surrounded by the palm trees, all designed and decked out by Ice. Right beside all the war machines that he heartily approved of. He grinned at her. "When are you coming over to visit?" His gaze went to Levi, raising his eyebrows back at her. "You guys should come over for a week or two or three."

"It's not a bad idea," Levi said. "We could use a long holiday, just not yet."

"That sounds familiar." Bullard grinned. "Anyway, I'm off. We'll hit the airport and then pick up the plane and head home." He added, "As always, call if you need me."

Everybody raised a hand as he returned to the helicopter and his buddy who was flying him to the airport. Ice had volunteered to shuttle him there, but he hadn't wanted to take her away from her family or to prolong the goodbye. He hopped inside, waving at everybody as the helicopter lifted. Two of his men, Ryland and Garret, were in the back seats. They always traveled with him.

Bullard would pick up the rest of his men in Australia. He stared down at the compound as he flew overhead. He preferred his compound at home, but damn they'd done a nice job here.

With everybody on the ground screaming goodbye, Bullard sailed over Houston, heading toward the airport. His two men never said a word. They all knew how he felt about Ice. But not one of them would cross that line and say anything. At least not if they expected to still have jobs.

It was one thing to fall in love with another man's woman, but another thing to fall in love with a woman who was so unique, so different, and so absolutely perfect that you knew, just knew, there was no hope of finding anybody else like her. But she and Levi had been together way before Bullard had ever met her, which made it that much more heartbreaking.

Still, he'd turned and looked forward. He had a full roster of jobs himself to focus on when he got home. Part of him was tired of the life; another part of him couldn't wait to head out on the next adventure. He managed to run everything from his command centers in one or two of his locations. He'd spent a lot of time and effort at the second one and kept a full team at both locations, yet preferred to spend most of his time at the old one. It felt more like home to him, and he'd like to be there now, but still had many more days before that could happen.

The helicopter lowered to the tarmac, he stepped out, said his goodbyes and walked across to where his private plane waited. It was one of the things that he loved, being a pilot of both helicopters and airplanes, and owning both birds himself.

That again was another way he and Ice were part of the same team, of the same mind-set. He'd been looking for another woman like Ice for himself, but no such luck. Sure, lots were around for short-term relationships, but most of them couldn't handle his lifestyle or the violence of the world that he lived in. He understood that.

The ones who did had a hard edge to them that he found difficult to live with. Bullard appreciated everybody's being alert and aware, but if there wasn't some softness in the women, they seemed to turn cold all the way through.

As he boarded his small plane, Ryland and Garret following behind, Bullard called out in his loud voice, "Let's go, slow pokes. We've got a long flight ahead of us."

The men grinned, confident Bullard was teasing, as was his usual routine during their off-hours.

"Well, we're ready, not sure about you though ..." Ryland said, smirking.

"We're waiting on you this time," Garret added with a chuckle. "Good thing you're the boss."

Bullard grinned at his two right-hand men. "Isn't that the truth?" He dropped his bags at one of the guys' feet and said, "Stow all this stuff, will you? I want to get our flight path cleared and get the hell out of here."

They'd all enjoyed the break. He tried to get over once a year to visit Ice and Levi and same in reverse. But it was time to get back to business. He started up the engines, got confirmation from the tower. They were heading to Australia for this next job. He really wanted to go straight back to Africa, but it would be a while yet. They'd refuel in Honolulu.

Ryland came in and sat down in the copilot's spot, buckled in, then asked, "You ready?"

Bullard laughed. "When have you ever known me *not* to be ready?" At that, he taxied down the runway. Before long he was up in the air, at cruising level, and heading to Hawaii. "Gotta love these views from up here," Bullard said. "This place is magical."

"It is once you get up above all the smog," he said. "Why Australia again?"

"Remember how we were supposed to check out that newest compound in Australia that I've had my eye on? Besides the alpha team is coming off that ugly job in Sydney. We'll give them a day or two of R&R then head home."

"Right. We could have some equally ugly payback on that job."

Bullard shrugged. "That goes for most of our jobs. It's the life."

"And don't you have enough compounds to look after?"

"Yes I do, but that kid in me still looks to take over the world. Just remember that."

"Better you go home to Africa and look after your first two compounds," Ryland said.

"Maybe," Bullard admitted. "But it seems hard to not continue expanding."

"You need a partner," Ryland said abruptly. "That might ease the savage beast inside. Keep you home more."

"Well, the only one I like," he said, "is married to my best friend."

"I'm sorry about that," Ryland said quietly. "What a shit deal."

"No," Bullard said. "I came on the scene last. They were always meant to be together. Especially now they are a family."

"If you say so," Ryland said.

Bullard nodded. "Damn right, I say so."

And that set the tone for the next many hours. They landed in Hawaii, and while they fueled up everybody got off to stretch their legs by walking around outside a bit as this was a small private airstrip, not exactly full of hangars and tourists. Then they hopped back on board again for takeoff.

"I can fly," Ryland offered as they took off.

"We'll switch in a bit," Bullard said. "Surprisingly, I'm doing okay yet, but I'll let you take her down."

"Yeah, it's still a long flight," Ryland said studying the islands below. It was a stunning view of the area.

"I love the islands here. Sometimes I just wonder about the benefit of, you know, crashing into the sea, coming up on a deserted island, and finding the simple life again," Bullard said with a laugh.

"I hear you," Ryland said. "Every once in a while, I wonder the same."

Several hours later Ryland looked up and said abruptly, "We've made good time considering we've already passed Fiji."

Bullard yawned.

"Let's switch."

Bullard smiled, nodded, and said, "Fine. I'll hand it over to you."

Just then a funny noise came from the engine on the right side.

They looked at each other, and Ryland said, "Uh-oh. That's not good news."

Boom!

And the plane exploded.

Find Bullard's Battle (Book #1) here!

To find out more visit Dale Mayer's website.

smarturl.it/DMSRyland

Damon's Deal: Terkel's Team (Book #1)

Welcome to a brand-new series from *USA Today* best-selling author Dale Mayer, where dark-ops SEALs have special senses and skills, needed to solve intrigue, betrayal, and … murder. A series with all the elements you've come to love, plus so much more, … including psychics!

ICE POURED HERSELF a coffee and sat down at the compound's massive dining room table with the others. When her phone rang, she smiled at the number displayed. "Hey, Terk. How're you doing?" She put the call on Speakerphone.

"I'm okay," Terkel said, his voice distracted and tight.

"Terk?" Merk called from across the table. He got up and walked closer and sat across from Levi. "You don't sound too good, brother. What's up?"

"I'm fine," Terk said. "Or I will be. Right now, things are blown to shit."

"As in literally?" Merk asked.

"The entire group," Terk said, "they're all gone. I had a solid team of eight, and they're all gone."

"Dead?"

Several others stood to join them, gathered around Ice's phone. Levi stepped forward, his hand on Ice's shoulder. "Terk? Are they all dead?"

"No." Terk took a deep breath. "I'm not making sense. I'm sorry."

"Take it easy," Ice said, her voice calm and reassuring. "What do you mean, *they're all gone?*"

"All their abilities are gone," he said. "Something's happened to them. Somebody has deliberately removed whatever super senses they could utilize—or what we have been utilizing for the last ten years for the government." His tone was bitter. "When the US gov recently closed us down, they promised that our black ops department would never rise again, but I didn't expect them to attack us personally."

"What are you talking about?" Merk said in alarm, standing up now to stare at Ice's phone. "Are you in danger?"

"Maybe? I don't know," Terk said. "I need to find out exactly what the hell's going on."

"What can we do to help?" Ice asked.

Terk gave a broken laugh. "That's not why I'm calling. Well, it is, but it isn't."

Ice looked at Merk, who frowned, as he shook his head. Ice knew he and the others had heard Terk's stressed out tone and the completely confusing bits and pieces coming from his mouth. Ice said, "Terk, you're not making sense again. Take a breath and explain. Please. You're scaring me."

Terk took a long slow deep breath. "Tell Stone to open the gate," he said. "She's out there."

"Who's out there?" Levi asked, hopped up, looked outside, and shrugged.

"She's coming up the road now. You have to let her in."

"Who? Why?"

"*Because,*" he said, "she's also harnessed with C-4."

"Jesus," Levi said, bolting to display the camera feeds to the big screen in the room. "Is it live?"

"It is, and she's been sent to you."

"Well, that's an interesting move," Ice said, her voice sharp, activating her comm to connect to Stone in the control room. "Who's after us?"

"I think it's rebels within the Iranian government. But it could be our own government. I don't know anymore," Terk snapped. "I also don't know how they got her so close to you. Or how they pinned your connection to me," he said. "I've been very careful."

"We can look after ourselves," Ice said immediately. "But who is this woman to you?"

"She's pregnant," he said, "so that adds to the intensity here."

"Understood. So who is the father? Is he connected somehow?"

There was silence on the other end.

Merk said, "Terk, talk to us."

"She's carrying my baby," Terk replied, his voice heavy.

Merk, his expression grim, looked at Ice, her face mirroring his shock. He asked, "How do you know her, Terk?"

"Brother, you don't understand," Terk said. "I've never met this woman before in my life." And, with that, the phone went dead.

Find Terkel's Team (Book #1) here!

To find out more visit Dale Mayer's website.

smarturl.it/DMSTTDamon

Author's Note

Thank you for reading Zack's Zest: Heroes for Hire, Book 23! If you enjoyed the book, please take a moment and leave a short review.

Dear reader,

I love to hear from readers, and you can contact me at my website: www.dalemayer.com or at my Facebook author page. To be informed of new releases and special offers, sign up for my newsletter or follow me on BookBub. And if you are interested in joining Dale Mayer's Reader Group, here is the Facebook sign up page.
https://smarturl.it/DaleMayerFBGroup

Cheers,
Dale Mayer

Your THREE Free Books Are Waiting!

Grab your copy of SEALs of Honor Books 1 – 3 for free!

Meet Mason, Hawk and Dane. *Brave, badass warriors who serve their country with honor and love their women to the limits of life and death.*

DOWNLOAD your copy right now! Just tell me where to send it.

www.smarturl.it/DaleHonorFreeBundle

About the Author

Dale Mayer is a USA Today bestselling author best known for her Psychic Visions and Family Blood Ties series. Her contemporary romances are raw and full of passion and emotion (Second Chances, SKIN), her thrillers will keep you guessing (By Death series), and her romantic comedies will keep you giggling (It's a Dog's Life and Charmin Marvin Romantic Comedy series).

She honors the stories that come to her – and some of them are crazy and break all the rules and cross multiple genres!

To go with her fiction, she also writes nonfiction in many different fields with books available on resume writing, companion gardening and the US mortgage system. She has recently published her Career Essentials Series. All her books are available in print and ebook format.

Connect with Dale Mayer Online

Dale's Website – www.dalemayer.com
Facebook Personal – https://smarturl.it/DaleMayerFacebook
Instagram – https://smarturl.it/DaleMayerInstagram
BookBub – https://smarturl.it/DaleMayerBookbub
Facebook Fan Page – https://smarturl.it/DaleMayerFBFanPage
Goodreads – https://smarturl.it/DaleMayerGoodreads

Also by Dale Mayer

Published Adult Books:

Bullard's Battle
Ryland's Reach, Book 1
Cain's Cross, Book 2
Eton's Escape, Book 3
Garret's Gambit, Book 4
Kano's Keep, Book 5
Fallon's Flaw, Book 6
Quinn's Quest, Book 7
Bullard's Beauty, Book 8
Bullard's Best, Book 9

Terkel's Team
Damon's Deal, Book 1

Kate Morgan
Simon Says… Hide, Book 1

Hathaway House
Aaron, Book 1
Brock, Book 2
Cole, Book 3
Denton, Book 4

Harley, Book 14
The K9 Files, Books 1–2
The K9 Files, Books 3–4
The K9 Files, Books 5–6
The K9 Files, Books 7–8
The K9 Files, Books 9–10
The K9 Files, Books 11–12

Lovely Lethal Gardens
Arsenic in the Azaleas, Book 1
Bones in the Begonias, Book 2
Corpse in the Carnations, Book 3
Daggers in the Dahlias, Book 4
Evidence in the Echinacea, Book 5
Footprints in the Ferns, Book 6
Gun in the Gardenias, Book 7
Handcuffs in the Heather, Book 8
Ice Pick in the Ivy, Book 9
Jewels in the Juniper, Book 10
Killer in the Kiwis, Book 11
Lifeless in the Lilies, Book 12
Murder in the Marigolds, Book 13
Lovely Lethal Gardens, Books 1–2
Lovely Lethal Gardens, Books 3–4
Lovely Lethal Gardens, Books 5–6
Lovely Lethal Gardens, Books 7–8
Lovely Lethal Gardens, Books 9–10

Psychic Vision Series
Tuesday's Child
Hide 'n Go Seek
Maddy's Floor
Garden of Sorrow
Knock Knock…
Rare Find
Eyes to the Soul
Now You See Her
Shattered
Into the Abyss
Seeds of Malice
Eye of the Falcon
Itsy-Bitsy Spider
Unmasked
Deep Beneath
From the Ashes
Stroke of Death
Ice Maiden
Snap, Crackle…
Psychic Visions Books 1–3
Psychic Visions Books 4–6
Psychic Visions Books 7–9

By Death Series
Touched by Death
Haunted by Death
Chilled by Death
By Death Books 1–3

Broken Protocols – Romantic Comedy Series

Cat's Meow

Cat's Pajamas

Cat's Cradle

Cat's Claus

Broken Protocols 1-4

Broken and... Mending

Skin

Scars

Scales (of Justice)

Broken but... Mending 1-3

Glory

Genesis

Tori

Celeste

Glory Trilogy

Biker Blues

Morgan: Biker Blues, Volume 1

Cash: Biker Blues, Volume 2

SEALs of Honor

Mason: SEALs of Honor, Book 1

Hawk: SEALs of Honor, Book 2

Dane: SEALs of Honor, Book 3

Swede: SEALs of Honor, Book 4

Shadow: SEALs of Honor, Book 5

Cooper: SEALs of Honor, Book 6

Heroes for Hire

Diesel, Book 13

Jerricho, Book 14

The Mavericks, Books 1–2

The Mavericks, Books 3–4

The Mavericks, Books 5–6

The Mavericks, Books 7–8

The Mavericks, Books 9–10

The Mavericks, Books 11–12

Collections

Dare to Be You…

Dare to Love…

Dare to be Strong…

RomanceX3

Standalone Novellas

It's a Dog's Life

Riana's Revenge

Second Chances

Published Young Adult Books:

Family Blood Ties Series

Vampire in Denial

Vampire in Distress

Vampire in Design

Vampire in Deceit

Vampire in Defiance

Vampire in Conflict

Vampire in Chaos

Vampire in Crisis

Vampire in Control

Vampire in Charge

Family Blood Ties Set 1–3

Family Blood Ties Set 1–5

Family Blood Ties Set 4–6

Family Blood Ties Set 7–9

Sian's Solution, A Family Blood Ties Series Prequel
Novelette

Design series

Dangerous Designs

Deadly Designs

Darkest Designs

Design Series Trilogy

Standalone

In Cassie's Corner

Gem Stone (a Gemma Stone Mystery)

Time Thieves

Published Non-Fiction Books:

Career Essentials

Career Essentials: The Résumé

Career Essentials: The Cover Letter

Career Essentials: The Interview

Career Essentials: 3 in 1

Made in United States
Orlando, FL
22 May 2022

18088269R00124